The Lost Legacy

THE
LOST
LEGACY

Renate Chapman

Montlake
Romance

Text copyright © 1980 by Renate Chapman

Published by Montlake Romance
P.O. Box 400818
Las Vegas, NV 89140

ISBN-13: 9781477838174
ISBN-10: 1477838171

The Lost Legacy

CHAPTER I

Quietly they moved through my head in a veil of mist—little figures like marionettes—in and out, up and down, to and fro, all around. Came the appointed moment, the deed was done by one of them. Little marionettes that weren't marionettes at all but real people.

In my mind's eye, I had seen them often. Inexorably, they appeared, bidden or unbidden. I was haunted by the vision, and there was nothing I could do about it.

I came back to reality, which was fortunate, as I happened to be behind the wheel of a car moving over a scenic country highway. I shifted the car into low as the sharp turn approached, and mentally I shifted myself too. It was necessary. I had come to my journey's end and an entirely new set of circumstances faced me. Slowing, I made the turn.

How little it had changed—Jacob's Corner— the old house of faded red brick, two-storied, shuttered, with twin chimneys rising from the horizontal peak of the roof. The flowering crab apple trees still lined the drive that led to the garage. The huge old sycamore, with its mottled bark, still lent its dappled shade to the front lawn. Geraniums still sent out their crimson blossoms from the old stone urn beside the sidelighted front door.

You see such old houses in the country, I thought, parking the car. All too often they are crumbling into nothingness. But Jacob's Corner was intact and appeared to be rock solid.

Walking up to the front door, I felt almost as if I'd never been away, but only for a moment did I feel that way.

A calico cat curled at the base of the urn. It lifted its head, gave me an inquisitive look, then dismissed my presence with a cat's typical haughtiness. Stooping to pet the animal, I was pleased to be greeted with an agreeable purr. Perhaps that was a good omen, I thought.

My finger touched the doorbell quickly, lest I lose my nerve. I'd had doubts about this visit. Pro and con arguments had sparred inside me for some time before I made the final decision. I still didn't know whether I'd made the right decision or not. But it was very late in the game to be assailed by self-doubt.

The paneled door swung in.

"Oh, Miranda," Aunt Leslie said in her lively voice. "So you did come. How well you look! I think it'll be just wonderful for your grandfather. Should do him a world of good to see you." The animated woman who stood before me was crisply attired in a green print dress. Though she was in her forties, her face still had a round, girlish quality, and her prematurely gray hair was still shorn close around her head.

My Aunt Leslie hadn't changed very much. It surprised me. Sometimes people change drastically over a period of several years. She'd added a pound or two, but the honeyed words that hid you-never-knew-what were still the same, as were the green eyes you could never quite read.

I'd never been very fond of my aunt and hadn't known she'd be staying at Jacob's Corner when I was to be there. I'd hoped for privacy on my visit to the grandfather I had not seen in some six years.

"Oh, but you do look so good, Miranda," she went on.

"Thank you," I told her.

"Of course, at your age you should."

I gave her a vague smile and said, "You're looking well."

"Oh," Aunt Leslie said, brushing at something imaginary on the green foliage print of her dress, "time goes on. Dreadful thing, time."

"It heals," I said.

"Yes indeed—sometimes. Why, do come on in, Miranda. Don't just stand there. Daddy's anxious to see you."

Everything looked the same inside. What's

more, it smelled exactly as I remembered it. My sense of smell is a strong one and evocative of memories. It might have been yesterday....

My eyes swept the interior—the long central hallway, the cherry staircase just to my right, the living room to my left...opposite it, the den. The door was open, I noticed, and I felt a slight shiver. *That door...that room.*

I didn't glance into the den, although I stood very near to the doorway. That room had been an important part of the vision that had haunted me for the past several years, and I didn't care to begin my visit with a painful, graphic reminder of bygone days.

Leslie was continuing. "We've fixed up the back room downstairs as a bed-sitting room for Daddy. He's really not up to climbing stairs anymore, and it just isn't safe." She made a move to lead me down the hallway. Her hand brushed the newel post of the staircase as she moved along and approached the door beyond it.

"Whoa," a deep voice called down from above us.

I shot a glance up the stairs, where a man and woman were descending. A second twinge of disappointment stirred inside me. I had not known Uncle Walter and his wife Rita would be at Grandfather's either, and I had not been anxious to see them. I was no fonder of my father's brother and his wife than I was of Leslie.

"Long time no see," Walter said. "What are you up to, Miranda?"

A snappy rejoinder or two were on the tip of my tongue, but I responded politely. "Why, Uncle Walter, I'm visiting my grandfather."

"And you're all grown up. What a fine-looking young woman you've turned into," he continued.

"Isn't she attractive, though," Leslie said.

"Ah, youth," Rita murmured.

I myself murmured the appropriate responses, but my mind was sizing everyone up.

Walter and Rita hadn't changed greatly, either.

Like Leslie, Walter had added a few pounds, but he was still reasonably trim. His neat mustache, looking the same as always, still gave him a more distinguished look than I thought he really deserved. Touches of gray in his dark hair showed only at the temples. That wasn't necessarily a natural condition. And when he stood right before me, I decided there were faint signs of dissipation in his face that had not been apparent in earlier days. But, if you didn't look too closely, Walter still made a good impression as far as appearance was concerned. I didn't think I'd ever seen him untidy or soiled from honest labor.

Rita too had put on a few pounds, but I remembered her as a beanpole and the increase was something of an improvement. Her short and curly auburn hair still had a tousled look, and she was neatly turned out in a tailored pair of pants in hunter green and a silk shirt in a very soft olive green. She smelled of expensive perfume. She had always left a trail of fragrance behind her.

"I hope you're not doing the wrong thing,"

Walter said. "The old man's not in the best of health these days. I don't want to see him upset. I'm in bad shape myself, you know—back trouble."

"I'm sorry to hear that."

Walter, I remembered, had been in bad shape every now and then, during which time he usually managed an extended expense-free lodging at his father's. As it was with the little boy who cried wolf once too often, his complaints had not always been taken seriously. I had always found him exasperating and thought that I probably should continue to do so for as long as we both lived.

"Just don't say anything about *what happened,*" Rita suggested.

She called it *what happened.* I had come to think of it in terms of little marionettes.

I settled a look on her. "I have no intention of doing that."

"Miranda knows better," Walter said, smoothing his mustache.

"Of course she does," Leslie cooed. "And if Daddy brings up the subject, just steer him away from it. You always were a clever girl, Miranda. Just like your father."

Inwardly I sighed. I knew it would be a miracle if I made it through the day with my disposition unsullied.

It had not been my intention to greet Grandfather in the presence of the rest of the family. A private meeting would have been much preferred, under the circumstances. They all seemed intent.

however, on following me to his room, so I did not protest.

After a light tap and an immediate command from inside to enter, Leslie threw the door open.

Grandfather's hair was whiter than I remembered it, but my first impression was one of someone more robust than I had expected. His color was good. He'd always been ruddy-faced and now showed some signs of a suntan. Wrapped in a cardigan sweater—it was cool in the room—his frame was somewhat obscured, so I was not sure whether he was thinner. But he didn't look much thinner in the face. He had been reading a book and appeared comfortably settled in his favorite upholstered rocker, although an expectant look was evident on his face.

"Well, look who's here, Daddy," Leslie said.

Grandfather adjusted his glasses and peered at me. "I thought it was Miranda when I heard the doorbell," he said slowly. "I was just about ready to get up and go look for myself. Well, child, let me have a look at you."

"She's hardly a child, Daddy," Leslie continued.

I obliged him by moving closer to him. "Hello, Grandfather. How are you feeling?"

"I'm feeling pretty good today. I have good days and bad. But just in case, I check the obituary every day to see whether I died or not."

"Oh, don't talk that way," Leslie protested. "You know you're good for at least another twenty years."

He chuckled to himself, then changed his

expression and seemed to shiver. "If nothing else, I may freeze to death. Do we have to keep it so chilly in the house?"

"You're cold natured, Dad," Walter said. "You need to dress more warmly."

"I guess I'll have to find out what the Eskimos wear."

"Let me see what I can do." Leslie went to a closet built into one end of a paneled wall. In the center of the wall was a fireplace that had been blocked up at some indeterminate time in the history of the house. At the bottom of the closet were two drawers, one of which my aunt opened, pulling out a colorful afghan.

Grandfather grumbled but accepted her ministrations meekly. Then he turned his attention back to me. "What have you been doing with yourself, girl?"

"I've gone to school mostly, studying art."

"You always did like to draw, didn't you? You were real good at it, too."

"Maybe we'll have a famous artist in the family," Walter said.

"Like Joan Miro," Rita added. "She's famous, isn't she?"

Leslie pounced on the statement with alacrity, as if she wanted to beat me in correcting Rita. "It isn't pronounced that way, and she's a he."

"Well," Rita said with an indifferent toss of her curly head, "what difference does it make?"

"Did you bring along any of your artwork?" Leslie asked me. "We'd all love to see some of the things you've done."

"I'm afraid I didn't. But I brought along some of my paraphernalia."

Grandfather had wearied of the talk of art. He got to a meatier matter. "You're not married yet, girl?"

"No, Grandfather, I'm not," I said evenly. I probably could have been, I said to myself—a time or two. Somehow things had never quite jelled.

"Footloose and fancy-free," said Walter. "That's the way to be."

"Just like me," Grandfather said with a chuckle.

"I always thought you'd turn out to be a career girl," Leslie told me.

"My life isn't over yet," I reminded her.

For some reason Rita thought that was funny.

"No, of course not," Leslie replied. She changed the subject. "Perhaps we'd better leave Miranda with Daddy now. I know they must have a lot to say to each other."

Grandfather fussed with the afghan over his knees as the three of them were leaving the room.

"They all kind of get on a person's nerves sometimes, don't they?" he said to me when they were out of earshot.

"You know about that better than I."

"Oh—diplomat, aren't you? You're being kind, Miranda. You've been around them. I expect your memory's pretty sharp. They're affectionate and pretty good to me, but someday I'll be gone and everything'll be left to divvy up. I reckon that'll make my passing a little easier for them to take."

Sometimes it's better not to comment. I thought this was one of those times.

Grandfather was silent for a while; a telltale, faraway look came into his eyes.

I knew what he was going to say before he said it.

"How—how is Richard these days?"

"So-so," I replied quietly. "Dad's health's good and his business is sound. Mother is well." Actually, things were rosy—in most respects, but not one.

Grandfather nodded.

What went on behind the faded blue eyes? What did he feel? Remorse? Anguish? Indifference? I didn't think it was the latter. He wasn't quite ready to reveal himself just yet, but his asking about my father had been a signal to me that time had brought somber reflections to the man. I had rather suspected that already, however. Otherwise, why would he have asked me to come?

"And you must make him proud, Miranda."

"Well, I—"

"What an odd name they gave you. I never did know why they named you that exactly."

"It was Mother's idea. She had seen an awfully good production of *The Tempest* before I was born. And she loved the actress who played Miranda."

"Women are like that. Of course, I don't think your grandmother would have done anything like that. That play had one of happily-ever-after endings, didn't it? Not like all those things where everyone gets stabbed or poisoned in the end. I saw it on television once. Didn't see too much sense in it. Don't know why I even watched. Guess there wasn't anything else on. Well, girl, I'm glad you came. Did you drive down?"

"Yes, Grandfather."

"Independent like all women these days, aren't you? Your grandmother wouldn't have done that, either."

"I do what I please, mostly."

"That's the Calvin blood in you. Were you surprised when I wrote you, girl?"

"Yes, I think I was."

"Bet you didn't know where I got your address."

I admitted it. "I had no idea at all."

He smiled to himself. "Do you remember Doug Lassiter?"

"Yes, of course I remember him." I remembered him very well. He'd been a little older than I, a cocky, arrogant boy. It sounds as if I didn't care very much for anyone around Jacob's Corner, I know. But I'd never been able to find any affection in my heart for Doug.

"Doug got it for me. He went to the library. You know how they keep phone books from all over the country. Well, he looked it up. There was just one listing for Calvin in the Chicago book with Richard's middle initial. We took a chance on it being the right one."

"Very clever."

"Well, a thing's only clever if it works. If it doesn't work, it was a danged fool idea."

I smiled. "So Doug was in on it?"

"Yes. I see him now and then. I talked it over with him. I didn't want to say anything around here. Doug thought it was a good idea. So if your visit turns out good, you can thank him. If it turns out the other way, you can blame him."

"You know how to work things out, don't you, Grandfather?"

"I give it a try." He thought a moment then. "I didn't know if you'd be living at home or not. Figured you might be out by yourself, all independent like."

"No, I'm still living at home."

"That's where you belong. It's a wicked world, child, no place for a girl to be out by herself."

He's mellowed, I thought to myself after our little chat.

In the Calvin family, unlike that of *The Tempest,* no happily-ever-after ending had occurred—yet. It would seem that Grandfather now had thoughts of remedying that situation. But could he? It had been several years now, and still the truth of what happened that day was not known. Perhaps we would all go to our graves not knowing what had happened, who had committed the deed.

But somewhere someone knew. It was very possible that it was someone at Jacob's Corner right now. I gave a little shudder when I realized that I was perhaps sharing a home with a murderer.

CHAPTER I

"I fixed up the little back room for you," the housekeeper said. "The others have a permanent claim on the two forward bedrooms."

I was glad Nina Symmes was still keeping house for Grandfather. Nina I liked. She had come to Jacob's Corner when Grandmother's health had begun to fail, a year or so before...before what happened.

Nina was truly a nondescript middle-aged woman. Makeup and fashion weren't her interests, and her short, graying hair fell in the waves that nature had decreed. A slightly bulbous nose seemed at first glance to mar her features, but once one came to know her, it seemed a relatively minor flaw. She was efficient, a no-nonsense, take-charge person. If she had any vice besides a taste for fancy chocolates, I had never heard about it.

Foremost among her virtues was that she got on very well with Grandfather, who wasn't always an angel to deal with. In my experience, no Calvin was. But under Nina's tutelage I had seen him more than once turned as meek as a lamb.

"I use the room on the other side now," she told me. She meant the second room on the left side of the upstairs hall, just opposite the one she was showing me now. Once she had occupied the room right beneath my present one—the room that now served as Grandfather's bed-sitting room.

In back of the house, two rooms—serving as a kitchen and a utility room—had been added at a later date to the original structure. The original structure, however, stood foursquare. And the upper story had two front rooms on opposite sides of a central hall, and two back rooms. The forward bedrooms were larger and better furnished than the back two.

The room Nina now occupied had lost a chunk of space where a small series of steps leading to the attic were enclosed along the south wall, the one that faced the river behind the house.

The room I was to occupy had been quite chopped up, losing its southeast corner when the amenity of a bath had been added at some later date. It hadn't done anything for the proportions of the room, but sometimes the esthetic must give way to the practical.

"The others are in and out all the time," she was saying. "Leslie comes for regular, brief visits. But

Walter—" She left the sentence unfinished, assuming that I didn't need to be told about Walter.

"I'd just as soon have this little room," I told her. "You can see the river from here." Immediately I walked to the window that faced the back lawn. Down below I could see the silver ribbon of the Ohio beyond the wooded slope upon which the house sat. And beyond the river was the State of Kentucky.

"I'm like you," she said with something of a sigh. "Sometimes I just watch the river for the longest time…when there's no work to be done."

"It is fascinating, the river." I moved to the window on the west and looked out over the modern, two-car garage and the drive lined with crab apple trees. A little farther away was the familiar little toolshed near the vegetable patch, a very modest affair now.

"I cleaned everything yesterday," Nina said.

"You didn't need to bother. I won't be busy. I could have done it myself."

She'd even put a rose in a bud vase, I noticed with pleasure.

I walked then to the north wall, the paneled fireplace wall with a built-in closet just to the left of the fireplace. Like the one below, this fireplace had been blocked up by earlier tenants, probably in a burst of enthusiasm over central heating. In fact, the fireplace in the den was the only one in the house in working order.

The paneled wall had been given a coat of gray paint fairly recently. It looked well with the striped paper that had been on the other walls for many years, but I absently wondered what kind of wood was under the layers of paint.

I touched a finger to the paneling. "This really is an old house, isn't it, Nina? I've heard it estimated to be a hundred and fifty years old. Of course, there are much older houses in this country. And in Europe it's not old at all. Still—"

"I wouldn't know about that," she said briskly. "But my experience is that people exaggerate a lot when it comes to things being old. It's fairly old, though. I think it was standing when my great-grandmother was a girl."

That was right. Nina was a local whose family had lived in the area for generations, longer than the Calvins had. She had been away from the area for a number of years before returning and going to work for Grandfather. I believed she had had a brief marriage when young. It had been an unhappy union, and she hadn't gone that route again.

Probably Nina's local origins aided her in her relationship with Grandfather. She had known him—and she knew other people who had known him—in his salad days.

Nina was continuing. "That was probably before the sisters lived here. It's probably been standing a good hundred years."

"You think so, huh?"

"If a thing's not new, it's best for it to be real old—antique. Antique, antique, everything's antique suddenly. Now all that is just my unexpert opinion. You be sure and let me know if you need anything."

"I don't think I will, but thank you, Nina."

Perhaps she was right, but Grandfather thought the house was older than that. It had withstood the years with a good deal of grace, which Grandfather had attributed to craftsmanship. Of course, upkeep had counted for something.

But more than once I had heard Grandfather say, "The man who built this house knew exactly what he was doing." In any event, distinctively Federal touches did abound. The built-in cherry cupboard in the den was magnificent, with nothing of the Victorian grandiose to mar it.

It took my mind off unpleasant matters to speculate about the origins of Jacob's Corner.

No one seemed to know who Jacob was. Time devours so much of history. People live and die and are forgotten, along with their deeds. No one even knew if it was a first name or a surname, whether Jacob was the craftsman who fashioned the house, or just another of its temporary tenants.

He must have pulled some weight, I thought. His name had affixed itself with a solid permanence.

What I did know was that, previous to Grandfather's ownership, two deeply religious, reclusive sisters had lived in the house for about fifty years. For the most part, they had shunned the outside world, but fortunately they had kept the house clean and in good repair. Fifty years is a long time. Whatever they knew about the history of Jacob's Corner had died with them.

Grandfather had owned the house for nineteen or twenty years, purchasing it during the days when he ran his hardware shop. He had sold his business and retired before the unhappy event of earlier years.

It seemed a shame more wasn't known about the history of Jacob's Corner. There had to be some history there.

If it were one hundred and fifty years old, it would have been standing before the Civil War. It would have been built at a time of great growth and also a time of great division and turmoil in this country. Northward the house had faced the growing industrial expansion of that section of the country. Behind the house had curled the busy Ohio, with its packets and barges and steamships, and beyond it the southern states.

Yes, I thought, the house had probably seen a great deal of history being made.

My thoughts turned to other matters then. The little room looked much the same as the last time I had seen it. A faded chenille spread, once a deep rose and now a softer shade, covered a walnut spool bed. The rest of the furniture was oak—an old rocker with bentwood arms and a bureau. A Grandma Moses print still hung over the bed.

I walked to the bureau, with its tilting oval mirror and handkerchief drawers, and leaned over, first of all, to smell the red rose in the vase. Then I studied the reflection in the mirror.

Outwardly, I hadn't changed greatly myself since the last time I was here. The dark hair that fell from a center part was a little shorter now, shoulder length. My deep gray eyes were probably my most striking feature. Of course, I had matured, but I still had the slender frame of those earlier days.

I had changed inside, though. The harsh realities of life had come to me early, and they had left their mark. Not everyone at sixteen is a star witness at the murder trial of her own father. Then there were the several years of exile my parents and I had endured.

Gazing into the mirror, I wondered what this visit had in store for me. There were feelings stirring inside me that begged for a label. I resisted, because the terms that verged on my tongue had to do with foreboding . . . *omen* . . . *presage* . . . *portent.*

CHAPTER III

I'd gone down to the car and carried my own luggage upstairs, not wanting anyone to suggest that Walter do it. Not that anyone was too likely to suggest that Walter do anything resembling work. Besides, he had already mentioned his bad back, hadn't he? After lugging the pieces up the stairs, I had unpacked my clothes and stayed put until Leslie came to the door announcing dinner.

The dining room was on the left half of the house, between kitchen and living room. Approaching it, I walked through the living room and paused just to glance around a moment or two.

The room looked the same as it always had, the same chintz-covered sofa, the same furniture arrangement, the same pressed glass candlesticks and little bisque figures on the mantel of the closed-off fireplace.

The dining-room furniture was mahogany, not new and not terribly old. Lace curtains hung at the window, and the big oblong table was covered with a lace cloth.

One change I noticed was that the noisy air conditioner in the living-room window had been replaced by central air conditioning.

Grandfather, still in his cardigan sweater, occupied the head of the table, as he always had. He still used his special cup and fork, which he demanded no matter what the occasion or what kind of table service was used. He might have mellowed but in many ways he hadn't changed a whit.

Walter sat to the left of his father, as memory told me he had always done.

I gave them all time to take their accustomed places before I sat down at one of the remaining chairs.

Since returning, I had been subject at moments to a wave of disbelief, the sudden sensation that I had to be dreaming. I wasn't really back at Jacob's Corner, back with the people who had treated me and my parents, especially my father, very shabbily. But here I was; I wasn't dreaming at all.

Now there was a surface feeling of friendliness and kinship, which I wasn't sure I trusted. I had come to see Grandfather because he had asked me to, and he was old, not so well, and possibly not too long for the world. But I had not been anxious to associate with any of the others. I wondered if it was just an accident that they all managed visits to coincide with my own. Fat chance.

Nina brought in a big platter of barbecued chicken.

"It always was one of your favorites, wasn't it?" Leslie asked. "I hope you still like it."

"Yes, I still do," I told her.

"Messy to eat, though," she added.

"So what?" Walter asked. "This is home. We can eat any way we want. Can't we, Dad?"

Grandfather had never been one for niceties. He was busily tucking his napkin under his chin when he spoke. "Never had much use for etiquette—a lot of fool rules. Of course, we can eat any way we want."

Leslie smiled indulgently. She looked cool in a sleeveless dress of blue linen, her green eyes hiding so well whatever things were on her mind.

After a brief silence, Rita spoke. "I suppose you'll get awfully bored out here, Miranda. It's such a change from Chicago, isn't it?" Rita generally tried to outdazzle everyone else. Tonight she wore white slacks under a tunic top of gold and orange, with loose, billowing sleeves.

"No, I don't think I'll get bored. I lead a quiet life at home, spending lots of time sketching and painting. I'll do some sketching here. There's a lot of scenery."

"Oh? Think you'll be staying on for a while?" Rita inquired.

I surmised they were all curious to know how

long I was going to stay, but only Rita had the gumption—or the bad taste—to come right out and ask. "I really don't know," I told them all.

"Of course, she doesn't. She just got here," Grandfather said.

"You're not working then?" Walter asked.

"I've worked part-time for a department store for quite a while, doing fashion sketches for advertising. But they can get along without me for a time."

"Oh, that sounds exciting," Rita said.

Frankly, it was a bore to me, but I rephrased my thoughts before speaking. "It's not exactly what I had really wanted to do."

"Oh, Miranda probably wants to have her own little studio and spend her time painting for wealthy clients," Leslie said, and added, "A very worthy ambition."

There was something in the tone of her voice that struck me with force. Then I noticed Walter seemed to wear a pained expression.

Something became clear. I had been naive not to realize it sooner. They feared I had come to wheedle money out of Grandfather.

The absurdity of it! Money had never been on my mind when I'd tried to decide whether to make the trip. Grandfather had invited me; I had not invited myself.

I turned to silently eat my chicken, but my mind dwelled on thoughts of avarice.

On further reflection, it struck me that their resentment probably ran deeper than I had at first imagined. The inevitable acrimony over the divison of estates of parents was involved. During the earlier bitterness, Grandfather had said that Dad would not get a cent from him. My father had never indicated any interest in preserving his own third, but something told me Leslie and Walter would have a keen interest in preventing their present one-half from dwindling to one-third.

I became convinced they believed we were making overtures to Grandfather, Dad and I, in the hope of getting Dad written back into the will, in addition to capturing any morsels Grandfather might be inclined to throw my way. I hadn't the faintest notion whether Grandfather had provided for his grandchildren in his will.

I simply didn't care. I had seen this kind of bitterness encompass other families, bringing out the worst in everyone. The last thing on my mind was to encourage it in my own family, but there was little I could do if they preferred to harbor suspicions.

Thrusting such thoughts aside, I decided I'd better be congenial for the time being and asked Leslie about her sons.

"John's working on his master's and Eric will be a senior this year at Miami." She followed up that preamble with a detailed discussion about the progress of her sons over the past few years.

"They hardly ever get over to see me," Grandfather protested at the conclusion of her dissertation.

"You know how busy they are, Daddy," Leslie said smoothly, "working in the summer, school in the winter."

"If I had children, I'd see that they paid the proper respect," Walter said.

"But you don't have children," was Leslie's reply.

It was well Walter had married a bit late in life and had not had a family. He'd never have been one to sit up with a sick child at night, or to make any of the sacrifices parents must make at times. But, of course, that did not preclude his giving advice to others.

"We always know what other people ought to do," Grandfather said, apparently to the world at large.

Leslie took a more restrictive view. "Yes, people do. Usually the ones who have the least right to talk." Her green eyes darted a glance which caromed off Walter.

Walter was complacent. He touched a fingertip to his mustache. "I don't believe in mincing words. When I see something that isn't the way it should be, I say something about it."

There had always been a sort of love-hate relationship between Leslie and Walter. They were close in age, Leslie being the middle child while Walter was the youngest. Quick to defend each other against attack from outsiders, they nevertheless cut each other down at little provocation.

They were alike in many ways, having so much more in common than either one had with my father. Self-preservation, I think, was the force that dominated both their lives. Even as a girl I had sensed the calculating, look-out-for-number-one quality in each—and had never quite trusted either one.

"I think Walter is right." Rita had to get her two cents' worth in.

All this bickering was old hat to Grandfather. He put a quick end to the matter. Untucking his napkin, he said, "I'm ready for some of that chocolate cake Nina was making. Let's go to the den. It's time for the news." When it was time for the news, the world stopped spinning for Grandfather. He hadn't changed in that respect, either.

I volunteered to help Leslie with the cake and coffee, in order that Nina could commence work on the dinner dishes. After a mundane discussion of sizes of pieces and whether anyone would want ice cream, we prepared the trays and were ready to carry them into the den.

A shiver passed through me as I passed through the door and into the room, but the sensation soon receded. There was little reason for me to feel shivery about the room. What had happened had happened, but it had been years before. I had not been involved, nor had my father.

But a man had been killed in this very room. The murder had never been solved. I could not help wondering if the dead man's spirit lingered still. They say that spirits linger in houses where people have died a violent death. I had never personally known of such a happening, however.

I wondered parenthetically how long it had been before the others had felt comfortable in the room.

The den was little changed. I seemed to

remember all the details. There was an attractive Adam-style mantel in here. It sat in the middle of the wall that adjoined the room Grandfather now used as his bed-sitting room. To the left of the fireplace was a big handsome built-in cupboard occupying the corner that rose from floor to ceiling. About a third of the way up, an open, arched shelf held assorted pottery and items Grandfather had cherished. The lower section of the cupboard was enclosed with double doors.

While I glanced around the room, something different caught my eye. There was now a small braided rug in front of the fireplace, instead of the brown fluffy one that was burned into my memory.

I took my cake and coffee and sat at one end of the old leather sofa. Rita sat in the middle, and Leslie sat at the other end. Grandfather was in his favorite recliner that faced the television set, and Walter had taken a rocker by the fireplace.

The evening news offered topics of conversation. The Calvins were opinionated people and expressed their views freely most of the time. At one point in the news a young liberal politician made a speech about improving prison conditions. Grandfather and Walter, who could be surprisingly conservative at times, lambasted him.

"I don't think he's so bad," Rita said innocently. "He's good-looking, and such a sharp dresser."

No one deigned to comment. Grandfather and Walter acted as if she hadn't spoken. Leslie raised her neatly plucked brows.

At times I wondered if Rita was as simple-minded as she seemed, or if much of it was just an act, perhaps in the mistaken belief that women have to be stupid to appeal to men. In some ways she was more enigmatic than Leslie or Walter.

Things settled down.

Walter poured a little brandy for himself and Grandfather. Leslie and Rita seemed to have developed a mutual interest in the latest swimsuit styles (they wouldn't be caught dead in them, but found them worthy of lengthy discussion).

I settled back, a little dreamily. Then that day came back to me. It had been no dream; it had been a nightmare. I could see the little marionettes again.

CHAPTER IV

A Fourth of July gathering had brought us together that year.

Leslie, her husband Gregg, and their two sons had come over from Cincinnati. Dad, Mother, and I had come down from Chillicothe, where we lived at the time. Walter and Rita, newlyweds of some six months, had been at Jacob's Corner for several weeks—some malady had struck Walter. I don't remember what.

If a beginning to the story can be pinpointed, that is as close as I can come to it.

I must digress and explain further about Walter.

Most families have a Walter. To Walter, the grass is always greener elsewhere; somewhere down the road is the end of the rainbow, with its pot of gold. If he had set his mind to it, he could have been successful in a number of ways, but assiduous effort had always been beyond his ken.

His life had long since fallen into a pattern. First, he became involved with a promising job or moneymaking scheme, and he exuded optimism. Then the optimism waned, and soon he was out of work or out of prospects and, once again, a lodger at his father's home.

To those unacquainted with the more ironic facets of human nature it might seem reasonable to assume that a son like Walter would gain disfavor, while his hardworking siblings gained favor. In the parable, however, it was the return of the prodigal son that brought joy to the father's heart and resulted in an outpouring of love. It isn't so different today. And it wasn't so different with Grandfather. Richard and Leslie were strong and industrious and could take care of themselves. It was Walter who required the help, and Walter who got it, despite the fact that in financial deals Walter invariably lost more than he gained.

Enough about Walter.

Something had occurred that year before the others arrived en masse for the holiday. Perhaps that was the real beginning of the story.

Walter had been lured into participating in some sort of land speculation deal—I never knew the details. Having no ready cash, he was in the process of badgering his father for capital for the investment, and it was a substantial amount of money he was asking for.

When I was a youngster I had a habit of looking cross-eyed when I fibbed. Walter wasn't so obvious as that, but Dad had a way of telling when his brother was up to something. I think it was the jovial, jolly-good-fellow stance Walter assumed at such a time. It was always a dead giveaway.

When Dad had ferreted out the facts, he was furious. True to Calvin tradition, he wasn't one to mince words, either. He and Walter had a bitter row.

Then Dad went a step further.

The man who had persuaded Walter of the merits of the land deal was named Sam Roberts and was lodged at a motel in the nearby county seat. Dad sought out Roberts and a harsh confrontation took place in the motel lobby. In very direct language the man was warned to stay away from any and all Calvins. In addition, in the fury of the moment, Dad made an ill-advised threat.

A born salesman, persevering and undaunted, Sam Roberts insisted he would bring proof of the legitimacy of his financial plan out to the Calvin house. Dad told him not to bother. That was the day before the Fourth of July.

With relations strained almost to the breaking point, there was little celebrating of the Fourth at the Calvin household. Everyone muddled through the day as best he could.

The day after the Fourth dawned like any other day in July. It was hot, and to add to the discomfort, vestiges of bitterness remained.

Walter was particularly sulky. Naturally, Rita sided with Walter, and Leslie had also been goaded by Dad's harsh words into taking her younger brother's side, even though I doubt she had any faith in the business deal. Everyone else tried to stay out of the squabble.

Early that morning, Leslie's husband had returned, until the weekend, to Cincinnati and took along their two sons. Gregg had to return to work. The boys were sports enthusiasts and their softball league had a game scheduled.

By lunchtime, although none of us knew it, the gears had been set into motion for what was to come. We all played out our roles. Like marionettes, moving from place to place and performing our duties at the dictates of some unseen force.

I've gone over it so many times. In my imagination I can look down on the scene, as if it were a stage setting, and can place each character in the proper position. *They start to move...a mist moves in and obscures the view...something happens....*

Between one and one-thirty that day, my mother left the house and drove to a local dentist's office. On top of everything else, she'd lost a filling the day before and planned to have it replaced right away.

Walter had complained of fatigue after lunch and retired upstairs to the same room he now occupied, the first room on the left side of the hall.

Rita had taken a magazine and pulled a lawn chair out to the east side of the house, the left side in which the living room was situated. There was shade on that side. There was shade in other places, but for some reason she chose that location.

Grandfather had sought blessed solitude in a fishing jaunt to a favorite spot on the river, a spot about half a mile from the house. He'd walked down, following a woodland path.

Leslie, Nina, and Dad were scattered about at various points outdoors.

I had been bored. At age sixteen I had been very certain I would die if I could not think of something to do. I did think of something—a lukewarm idea, but better than nothing.

There was an old bicycle in the toolshed out by Grandfather's vegetable patch. I got it out and cleaned it up a bit, thinking I'd ride down the path and sit with Grandfather for a while. It was something to do.

At about this time the momentum seemed to quicken.

Grandmother had a caller, an old friend and one-time pastor, the Reverend Thomas Garrity. With him he brought his foster son, Douglas Lassiter, who had just returned home from school and some summer travel. Grandmother had whisked them to the living room, which at that time had the noisy window air conditioner going, providing relief from the July heat.

I had gone but a short distance when the chain slipped off the bicycle. Unable to get it back on, I began to push the bicycle back up the path.

As I approached the toolshed, I saw Dad, who'd been shambling around the vegetable patch and had decided himself to walk down to the river to have some quiet words with Grandfather. I called to Dad to see if he could help me.

It must have been at about this time that Sam
Roberts arrived at the house. By now Leslie was in
the front yard. After the man had identified
himself, she knew Dad would not want to speak
with him. Reluctantly, however, she led him to the
den, asked him to wait, and partly closed the door.

By now realizing the Reverend Garrity was a
guest in the house, Leslie stuck her head in the
door to the living room and greeted the man.
Meanwhile, Doug, who was no stranger to the
Calvins, had gone to the kitchen to get himself a
cold drink. Leslie said she'd be back in a few
minutes and went down the hall and out the back.

She spent a little time looking around for Dad,
then spotted us near the toolshed.

Sometime during these moments Nina went in
the front door and walked up the stairs, going
unnoticed, for Grandmother and the clergyman
had their backs to the doorway. Reverend Garrity
had brought along a large number of snapshots,
and he and Grandmother tried to find the best spot
for viewing them, deciding at length on the sofa
along the front-facing wall.

Because of the crab apple trees along the
driveway, neither Dad nor I had noticed the two
automobiles now parked there. Dad told Leslie
he'd be around presently, but his visage was stern
and he didn't bother to hide the displeasure he felt
at Sam Roberts's peremptory call. He seemed in
no hurry to go to the house, devoting himself
instead to the problem of the bicycle chain. I knew
he was mulling over his options in dealing with the
intruder.

Leslie returned to the house, went to the kitchen, and prepared a tray of lemonade and cookies, which she carried immediately to the living room. She seated herself across from the others in a position that put her in direct view of the door to the den, which—she later said—was now closed, whereas she had left it partly open. Only Leslie could see the door. Grandmother and the Reverend Garrity still sat on the sofa, and Doug sat on a chair at their right. These three, however, had a view of most of the staircase and part of the hallway.

Still, we moved along the prescribed course, marionettes all.

Dad puttered with the bike, finally deciding a new chain would have to be bought. We put the vehicle back in the shed. Dad cleaned his hands with a rag kept in the shed and used a nearby watering hose to rinse them.

I decided against walking down to where Grandfather was. And Dad and I walked directly up to the house. He was saying nothing now but grimly contemplated something while chewing on his lower lip.

Dad hesitated by the front door as I went inside and straight up the stairs to the little room. I had seen Reverend Garrity's car and had it in mind to escape the formality of such a call. Had I realized Doug was with him, I'd have been even less anxious for the visit, but that is another story.

My most vivid impressions are those of the next few moments.

I reached the top of the stairs. The sun's rays

slanted across the floor through the window at the end of the hall. Outside, a blue jay screamed and scolded. Nina was stepping into the bathroom just down the way. I opened the door and stepped inside the little room.

A short span of time passed before I heard pounding sounds from downstairs. And then it took but seconds for alarm to spring up in me.

"Roberts!" It was my father's voice calling out.

Well knowing my father's Calvin temperament, as well as the contempt he had for the man, I suddenly wondered if he were throwing him bodily out the front door.

As I came out of my room and reached the head of the stairs, I could see Dad pushing at the door to the den. Reverend Garrity, Doug Lassiter, Grand-mother, and Leslie were approaching the scene at their various paces.

The door gave way then, and assorted exclama-tions rang out. Leslie screamed.

My next impressions are vivid also. I shall never forget the scene that I beheld inside the door after I had galloped down the stairs. A large man lay sprawled facedown on the fluffy brown rug in front of the fireplace.

I stood staring at the scene with a kind of morbid curiosity. Images spring to mind: Leslie, wide-eyed; Grandmother, her hands clasped to her heart. The men were moving around and bending over the prostrate body—Dad with a kind of precision, Doug with agility, and the frail clergyman with measured deliberation.

At the time I gave no thought to why an ornate commemorative letter opener lay bent out of shape on the floor.

Then the scene was chaotic. Everyone seemed to be moving and talking at the same time.

I had assumed the man had fallen, or had suffered an attack. Later, all the others claimed such an initial assumption also. It took little time for a different verdict to be announced.

"Look, there's blood on the back of his head," someone cried.

"Can you feel his pulse?" another asked.

"My God!"

"I think he's dead. Why, he's been—"

Voices were saying things that had never been said at Jacob's Corner, at least not in my memory.

I had to admit, though ruefully, that it was Doug Lassiter—lank, long-haired, egotistical Doug—who seemed to take charge. "Don't touch anything else," he commanded curtly. "Someone call the police."

Then Doug was searching for clues and possible hiding places. He looked up into the fireplace chimney, behind the sofa. Then he turned to the big corner cupboard. One of the doors at the bottom was slightly ajar.

We all watched with a dread fascination as he opened it fully and looked inside. I think perhaps we all believed some miscreant might actually be hiding in there. It was large enough to hold someone. But no one was concealed within, and we seemed to breathe a sigh of relief in the aggregate. Doug checked the windows, two at the front and one on the west, and announced that they all had been locked.

I wasn't really surprised at all of this from Doug. Despite his shortcomings, I'd never doubted his intellect.

During Doug's search, Walter had come hustling down the stairs, sleepy-eyed, his hair on end; and Nina was soon scurrying down in his wake. She sucked in a deep draught of air, looked fearful, and wrung her hands at the sight of the body on the floor.

Walter blinked with apparent disbelief. Then he said to Dad, "You did it. You actually did it. You killed him."

Dad's response was succinct but viciously spoken. "I did no such thing!"

"Oh, you know he wouldn't do anything like that," Leslie said, her usual breezy manner badly dampened. "No one in the family would. Some outsider's come in and done it…or something."

Walter's mustache quivered, his eyes narrowed. Then he thought of something. *"Where's Rita?* Is she still out in the yard?" He dashed off to find her, and Doug was right on his heels. They did find her, snoozing like a baby in the lawn chair.

It took time for all the implications to sink in.

We were all turning the odd event around in our minds. The man had been struck down by a sharp blow to the back of the head. It was incredible to suppose he had done it himself. But how did the person responsible get out of the room? The door had been barred from the inside by the ornate letter opener thrust into a crack behind the doorway facing. The windows were locked from the inside. There had been no one hiding anywhere, and no other means of exit. *How did the person get out?*

It was a question that would perplex many people for a long time.

Grandfather returned from solitude to find bedlam. The police had arrived—state police and the sheriff and his minions. The technicians did their work, and others asked questions. And asked questions. And asked questions.

By my own calculations, excluding the locked-room aspect, it seemed virtually impossible for anyone at Jacob's Corner to have committed the deed. I knew my father hadn't done it, and he was, after all, the one person with a bone to pick with Sam Roberts.

The police, however, had only my word as to Dad's whereabouts during the minutes preceding the killing. To his discredit was the nasty scene at the motel lobby when Dad had made a direct threat of physical harm to the man and did so in the presence of several witnesses. I knew the Calvins said things in the heat of anger that they didn't really mean, but that didn't cut very much ice with the police or with the county prosecutor, who was new at the job and out for blood.

Dad was charged with first-degree murder. The prosecutor claimed malice and premeditation.

The following months we all survived, although I would like to blot them from memory.

Never in my life had I dreamed my father would

be on trial for murder and I would be the key witness for the defense. Who would suppose such a thing?

Physical evidence was scant. A poker from the fireplace set had been the weapon used, but all fingerprints had been wiped away. The ornate surface of the letter opener revealed no discernible prints. Beyond that, all our prints, except those of Doug and the Reverend Garrity, were all over the den. The room had been much used and Nina hadn't cleaned it thoroughly since all the family had arrived.

I held up very well. But I was telling the truth, after all. To a person who didn't know I was telling the truth, the prosecutor's theory made some sense.

That theory was that Dad had gone into the den and deliberately struck the man down. The door had never been barred from inside. Dad had bent the letter opener and made a show of trying to force in the door. Repeatedly, the prosecutor hammered away that my testimony and Leslie's— that no one had gone into the den or come out while she was seated in view of the door—was given by very close relatives of the defendant. The potentially impeccable witness, the Reverend Thomas Garrity, had not been in a position to see whether anyone went in or out of the door, and his failing hearing precluded overhearing conversation or noises that younger ears might have picked up.

The prosecutor had wrung us all out, including Doug, who had testified he thought he'd heard the murmur of vague, unidentifiable voices and a soft thump perhaps ten minutes or so before the body was found. He could not be more specific because of the thrumming of the air conditioner. When questioned as to what he had made of the thump, Doug, true to form, had infuriated the prosecutor by replying, "Naturally, I assumed it was someone being murdered in the den of Mr. Calvin's house."

One additional bit of testimony stood out. I thought it important, and apparently so did others.

Nina testified she had been out in the upstairs hall, near the steps, at one point during the critical period. Glancing down at the front door, she'd seen what appeared to be a man in brown through one of the glass sidelights. The view had been brief and somewhat blurred; she could offer very few specifics.

With Nina, the prosecutor had switched tactics, putting on his kid gloves. He drew a picture for the jury of an old family retainer who'd lied—with the very best of intentions—to save her elderly employers from anguish. While Nina was fond of my grandparents, the hypothesis was filled with exaggeration, from my standpoint.

The man in brown perplexed me still. No one had been wearing brown that day.

I think we were all in a state of shock throughout the time of the trial. It was one of those things that happen to other people, not to our family. It's very hard to accept some things, even while they're happening, even when they're all over.

The jury acquitted Dad. After the furious

prosecution, we had all begun to fear the worst. The outcome was something of a surprise, but a welcome one.

I won't spend very much time speculating about the reasons for the decision. Perhaps it was one specific thing. Perhaps it was a combination of the jury's believing Leslie, Nina, and me. And perhaps it is simply that with our system of justice a person does have a fighting chance, and juries do tend to be right more than they are wrong. In this case, I knew they were right.

There was now jubilation in the family, but it wasn't to last forever. It wasn't to last a week.

Harm had been done. Suspicion had reared its head among family members, and my grandparents had been badly hurt. Grandmother had been particularly vulnerable because of her fragile health. Less than three months after the trial, she died. It is possible her death would have occurred regardless; no one can say. Within the family, however, resentment against Dad grew, and he was openly accused of bringing on his mother's death.

That had been the last straw. We moved to Chicago, where Dad was fortunate enough to have a friend who took him into business. We put our lives back together as best we could. But we had remained in exile ever since.

Naturally, that grim period had haunted me over the years. I was haunted by the memory of the man lying in that state of dreadful immobility in the den. I was haunted by the impersonal work of the police technicians and the unrelenting questions. I was haunted by the picture in my mind's eye of little marionettes bustling about doing their strange bidding.

In addition, there was the knowledge that somewhere the killer was still free, if the person was still alive. I didn't believe the crime would ever be solved and more was the pity, because doubt of my father's innocence would always persist in that case.

The upshot of all this was that I had turned more and more to my art and had become somewhat withdrawn.

"You in another world, Miranda?"

"What?" I surfaced to the present.

Rita had a steady, sidelong gaze aimed at me. "This room does that to me sometimes," she said.

"What do you think about me?" Leslie asked. "I was right on the spot when it happened. It probably happened while I was sitting right across the hallway, talking and drinking lemonade. You were sleeping in the shade, nowhere near."

"I was sleeping in the shade unprotected," Rita said. "I shudder sometimes when I think that someone may have been sneaking around the house—the man in brown that Nina spoke of—and passed right by me. Why, what if I woke up and saw him? He might have murdered me on the spot."

Leslie shrugged. She was one whose interest in the close calls of others was none too great.

Rita turned to me. "You know the police have never made another arrest in the matter, don't you?"

"I'm sure I would have heard about it if they had."

"I don't suppose they ever will. It's frightening, isn't it? I mean, something like that happening right here, and not knowing who did it. They say a person who kills once will kill again."

Walter had tuned in to our conversation. "You don't have anything to worry about, Rita. You read too many detective stories. Somebody did what they wanted to do. Then they were satisfied. Nobody else is in danger."

"Well, I still don't like it. Sometimes I get the creeps in this house."

"I'm sure whoever did it is far away," Walter told her with a tone of finality.

It was a not-so-subtle slam at my father, but I said nothing. I was in no mood to spar with Walter. Not now. But I knew I didn't quite trust him. He had always been too eager to pin the blame on Dad.

As a matter of fact, I didn't trust Leslie, either. Or Rita.

I went up to my little room, somber and reflective.

A few sour notes had been sounded, but things had not gone as badly as I feared they might. Perhaps some of my anxiety over this trip had been misplaced. Come to think of it, I told myself, the way my family had treated my parents and me, it was they who should be nervous and upset, not I.

CHAPTER V

It was a miracle I did not dream of the little marionettes that night. I don't know what I dreamed about. It had been an extremely peaceful sleep. I woke with no unpleasant memories to a decidedly pleasant new day.

There is something about a dazzling, sunny morning with birds chirping and caroling that makes one think everything is right with the world. I could understand Browning's sentiments very well.

It was just past seven when I went down the stairs. A person seems to wake up early when he or she doesn't have to.

I'm not sure what made me pause at the foot of the stairs before the door to the den. Something did, and a cloud passed over my dazzling morning.

47

The door was ajar. I pushed it open and stood with my hand on the jamb. Last night I hadn't noticed it. The crack was still there, where the letter opener had been wedged. Phooey on the prosecutor! Dad said the door had been barred from inside—it had been.

Nina had tidied the room already and opened the draperies to admit light. The homey furnishings exuded hospitality and family camaraderie. But I was looking past surface things.

It both intrigued and agitated me still. How did it all happen?

Whatever had happened, it occurred during a period of about fifteen or twenty minutes. Sam Roberts had been seen in town between one and one-thirty that afternoon. The approximate length of time to drive out would have put him arriving at about the time Leslie said he did.

Of course, no one was looking at watches or clocks and checking the minute they made each move that day, so pinpointing movements at precise times was out of the question. It did eliminate the possibility, however, that the man had been killed much earlier.

Sam Roberts probably arrived at a little past one-thirty, and within about twenty minutes had been found dead in a room that appeared to afford neither egress nor entry.

Like a cat, I am curious. An unsolved mystery to me is something to be cleared up. Something I can't help eggs me on.

And in this mystery, something very personal was involved. Never would I stop wondering.

I stepped into the room and surveyed it critically, then pushed the door almost shut. With the passing of the first flutters of apprehension the night before, natural instincts took over. I became insatiably inquisitive. Somewhere in this room there was a clue, surely.

I went to the fireplace, kneeled down on the stone hearth, and looked up into the smoke-stained interior. Not that I need have bothered. It would have been impossible for anyone to have escaped up the chimney. That fact had been established.

The fireplace wall was paneled and the other walls were made of plaster, now papered and a bit the worse for wear, if one looked closely. The possibility of hidden panels had not been over-looked. The paneled wall had been checked over and pronounced solid, with every plank secured to the wall.

There had been no one hiding in the bottom section of the big corner cupboard. Doug had checked it that day in the presence of us all.

Nevertheless, I kneeled down once again and opened up one of the fine old cherry doors. There was so much stuff inside that one could hardly see the interior. Books, old dishes, and bric-a-brac filled the space. I set a few things out on the floor and ran my hand over the bottom and side of the enclosure. It seemed as solid as the Rock of Gibraltar.

Surely the culprit had gone out through the front window, and the window had been subse-quently locked. The locks were the common old metal types that required but a simple flick of the wrist to be closed.

I really couldn't say whether anyone had stepped over that day and quickly snapped one of the window locks on. The scene had turned to one of chaos and there was much movement in the room. No one claimed to have seen anyone lock the window, but almost anyone could have done it, including Doug, who had checked and pronounced them all secure.

Now, sitting there lost to the world, I lost track of time. I was deep in thought when what sounded like a faint creaking of a floorboard gave me a turn. I whipped around. It wasn't beneath some of the people here to be spying on me, and I would have relished knowing who it was.

Quickly moving to the door, I looked down the hall and across into the living room. Nothing moved. I could have been mistaken. I went back to the cupboard and put the items back inside before I left the den.

"Don't you just love mornings like this?" It was Leslie coming down the stairs and looking cheerful. "But I'd have thought at your tender age you'd have been sleeping in later than this."

"Almost any other time I guess I would have," I told her.

"Well, let's rustle up some breakfast, first of all. Daddy likes an early, hearty breakfast." She paused to tap at the door to Grandfather's room. "Everything all right?" she called, and he grunted in reply. "We'll have it on the table in a few minutes."

Nina had boiled eggs and now had bacon sizzling in a pan.

"Why don't you set three places," Leslie told me. "Walter and Rita don't stir till the morning's half over. I'll pour the juice. Let's see, I think we used up all the orange marmalade. I'll have to open a new jar. Daddy can't eat breakfast without his marmalade."

I feared the three of us—Leslie, Nina, and I—might fall over each other, but work proceeded smoothly enough, and my aunt, my grandfather, and I were soon seated at the kitchen table.

Leslie continued to bubble over with enthusiasm. "Isn't it just a gorgeous day, Daddy?"

Grandfather slowly and automatically buttered his toast before answering. "Too good to be cooped up in the house. I've got a mind to go out and bait a hook."

"Don't go traipsing off by yourself," Leslie told him.

"You told me yesterday I was good for another twenty years," he reminded her.

"But that's provided you take care."

"I may not be able to do everything I used to do, but I can still take the bone-marrow express down to the fishing hole."

"Of course, you can. But you know what a worrywart I am. I think you ought to indulge me, Daddy."

"I'll walk down to the river with you, if you don't mind. I'll take my sketchbook along," I said.

"I remember when you used to throw in a line yourself."

"Yes, I did. It's been a long time."

"Don't suppose you ever did learn to bait your own hook."

"No, Grandfather, I didn't."

He shook his head. "Women are all the same."

"Now, you don't hear us saying men are all the same, do you?" Leslie said.

Conversation continued in a light vein throughout the rest of breakfast.

A little later Grandfather gathered his fishing supplies and I gathered my art supplies, and we set off—past the garage, the toolshed. The toolshed and woodland path stirred memories. The last time I'd started down that path something dreadful had come to pass. But that was in the past, and I knew I shouldn't dwell on such things.

We poked along. There was a slope to the ground and I feared Grandfather might pitch forward. He didn't, however.

Amid the *caws* of crows and the *rat-tat-tat* of a woodpecker, we arrived at Grandfather's second favorite haunt, closer than the one where he had been that day years before. It was a kind of small inlet, quiet and shaded. To me, it seemed a perfect site, but of course, I was no angler.

I found a big rock to sit on and looked out over the great waterway, its surface rucked by a slight breeze. Cattails waded, in their persistent way, at the water's edge, and I could see the carapace of a turtle floating leisurely across the inlet.

I took out my sketchbook. My mind was preoccupied, and doodles were all that emerged from my moving fingers.

"What kind of things do you usually draw, girl?" Grandfather asked me while working with his fishing line.

"Oh, things that look like things. Landscapes, bridges, anything that appeals to me."

He made a sound of approval. "None of that modern stuff, huh? I don't like modern art. Never did. No sense to it. Wouldn't have it in my house, and wouldn't go to see it."

The opinionated Calvins!

"You're not alone, Grandfather. Many people feel the same way."

"That shows that the bulk of people have good sense, mostly."

I made a hint of a bow and thought better of any inflammatory remarks in support of those who appreciated the modern style.

"I most always say what I think," he continued.

"I know you do," I told him.

"My children are just like me—in that respect," he hastened to add.

"Your granddaughter's been known to speak her mind," I told him with a smile.

The truth was, his exiled child—my father—was like him in more ways than were the other two. Both were opinionated, spoke their minds, were decisive, but had their feet planted firmly on the ground. Plain, hard-working, solid citizens Dad and Grandfather were. And always honest—no ifs, ands, or buts.

Walter said what he thought, *unless* it was expedient not to do so. In many respects he was a diametric opposite of Dad and Grandfather. And

Leslie too spoke her mind as a rule, but she had a flair for evasiveness,*if* it suited her purpose. And she had "city ways" that were a world apart from her father.

"Tell me something, Miranda—that is, of course, if it isn't something you'd object to," he added with an unusual show of deference. He puttered around a bit. "Does Richard ever speak of me?"

"Of course. Did you think he had forbidden the mention of your name? That sort of thing went out with high-button shoes, Grandfather. Yes, he speaks of you some. And we speak of what happened."

What happened—that terrible phrase again.

"Well, you know, the more I think about it, the more it seems to me that what happened couldn't have happened. There just ain't no way. I know Richard never did it. You were telling the absolute truth, weren't you, girl?"

"Yes, Grandfather."

"He has a right to hate me, and to hate the others, too."

Knowing Grandfather as I did, I knew making that admission took a lot of nerve. He had mellowed.

"He doesn't hate you. He realizes the strain you were under, with Grandmother's passing on top of everything else. He can be very stubborn, though. Me, now, I'm a combination of the two—my father's stubbornness tempered with my mother's forbearance."

"I came from right stubborn stock myself. My

mama and daddy—you never knew them—they were both stubborn as mules, just plain pigheaded. Mama would have stood pat before a hurricane." He shook his head. "But it's a fool who doesn't change his mind. In my old age I've come to realize that. Some lessons are a long time learning."

I thought I could see the writing on the wall. Grandfather wanted to make amends, wanted the family back together again. And I thought it was a good idea and that my father would go along. I hoped Grandfather approached it cautiously with everyone. I feared Leslie and Walter would not rejoice at the smoking of the peace pipe. Surely another codicil would be added to Grandfather's will. They'd both come round in due time; meanwhile, however, consummate care needed to be taken.

I heard the crackle of dried woodland matter first, then saw the shadow crawl down over a little dollop of sun beside me. Walter, I suspected, moseying down to keep abreast of possible developments that might affect his finances.

Turning, I faced a stranger, however. I stared. I pondered. Then recognition bombarded me. So much went through my mind. "Doug Lassiter!" I said.

"Why, Miranda, you're all grown up. You haven't changed all that much."

"But you have. I didn't recognize you at first. You're heavier. Your hair's short. And the mustache changes your looks altogether."

He grinned a half grin, turning up the corner of his mouth on the left side. The grin hadn't changed. If there had been anything distinctive about Doug Lassiter, it had been that little quirk of a grin.

"I have added a little plaster to my bony slats," he said. "Do you approve of the mustache? I think it adds a touch of knight-errantry."

"Why, yes. I think you're right."

"Just what a lawyer needs!"

In my opinion, Doug Lassiter was much more likely to be errant than knight. Privately, I'd always considered him a knave, a rogue. But, of course, I'd known him at the end of his whining schoolboy days. Perhaps time had wrought a vast improvement…I'd soon have an idea or two about that.

"Still drawing pictures, I see," he said.

I glanced at the sketchbook. "I'm unproductive at the moment, but, yes, I still draw pictures, as you say."

"Doug's passed his bar exam now, Miranda," Grandfather volunteered.

"Really? Well, I am impressed. Reverend Garrity must be so proud."

Doug's expression changed very little. A twitch at the corner of his mouth slightly disturbed the line of his mustache. "He died a couple of years ago, Miranda."

I drew in a quick breath. "Oh, I'm so sorry. I didn't know. I mean—"

He smoothed it over. "Of course not. Don't, think another thought about it. What have you been up to? School, I suppose."

"Yes," I answered absently. "I've studied art."

I felt bad about the faux pas, but I simply had no idea.... Reverend and Mrs. Garrity had both been along in years when they had taken Doug in, much too old to adopt him. He'd been a homeless problem child, but now it appeared he might have turned out quite well. One did not breeze through bar examinations on the basis of looks or devastating charm or even knight-errantry.

He nodded. Now his blue eyes seemed to scrutinize me. They seemed full of questions. That was all right. I'd have some questions for him if I got the chance to ask them.

He said, "You've got me to thank in part for your presence here, you know."

"Yes, Grandfather told me of your clever sleuthing."

"If she doesn't like it here, she can blame you instead of me," Grandfather told him.

"Not like it here? Why, just look at the girl. She's looking like a country bumpkin in jeans and plaid shirt already."

We continued to chat, on safe subjects, until Grandfather stopped pinning his hopes on a fish dinner and we gathered up our belongings and headed for the house.

"You're staying for lunch, aren't you, Doug?" Grandfather asked as we neared Jacob's Corner.

"Yes, I managed to wheedle an invitation out of Leslie."

"Humph! Wheedle! She wouldn't let you get away. Thinks you'll drop a juicy tidbit of gossip about the courthouse claque, or maybe get a scoop on who's getting divorced or suing."

"I'm fresh out of juicy tidbits."

"She won't believe it," Grandfather declared. "You'd better think of something."

"I'll try."

"You two just get ready for lunch," Grandfather said when we had reached the house. "I'm going to wash up and see if it's fixed. If it isn't, I'll tell the womenfolk to get a move on. I'm ready to eat."

When Grandfather was out of earshot, Doug said, "I love that old codger. But thank God he lived most of his life before women's liberation."

I smiled crookedly and had to agree.

Fortunately, the food was ready, and we soon sat down to a pleasant luncheon. The salmon croquettes were tasty. Grandfather had his indispensable cup and fork. The conversation was light. Perhaps it was Doug's presence that improved the dispositions of everyone present.

After lunch, Doug and I strolled outside, where we could talk in privacy.

He said, "This is something, isn't it? Seeing each other after all these years. Well, I guess it hasn't been that many. But a person wonders. I didn't know if you were a lady marine or a short-order cook, or if you had a husband—"

I laughed lightly. "I'm just a poor, struggling art major looking for a niche in the world."

It was something seeing each other. A lot like old times. Perhaps too much. Almost it gave me a deja vu feeling—all of us at Jacob's Corner at the same time. Oh, it wasn't exactly the same. Two of the principals were no longer alive, and Dad was not present. But the innocence of those three was beyond dispute. All the possibles were still here.

"You've done well," I added.

"I've had my ups and downs—don't we all?"

"Yes, we do."

"How's Richard?" he asked.

"Trite as it sounds, he's fine. We've all done very well, all things considered."

His blue eyes were looking into mine then.

"Do you think about it very much, Doug? *What happened,* I mean?" *What happened.* It was a phrase on my mind a good deal—it and visions of little marionettes moving around in a maddening, unexplainable pattern.

"Naturally, I think about it."

"What do you think about it, if I may be so presumptuous?"

"You presumptuous?" He took his time. The lawyer in him was coming out. He spoke cautiously. "I think something very strange happened. Somewhere there must be a key, but so far no one has found it."

"And it will never be found?"

He shrugged.

"I've thought of that myself," I said. "Somewhere there's a clue that's been overlooked. If we followed through on it, it would open up the way for the solution of the mystery. Just like in the detective stories, I guess. There's always something—usually something very minuscule—that puts the detective on the right track."

"I'm not a detective, Miranda. And I'm no Perry Mason."

"But you're trained in logic. Surely you've

deduced something. After all, you were on the scene. Ordinarily, the lawyer has to ferret, second guess, play the psychologist, trick, connive—"

"Here now," he said, with a quick half grin. "You're getting too close for comfort."

I persisted, the Calvin in me coming out. "You have to have drawn some conclusions. I know you have. If there was only one clear-cut deduction you could make from the entire affair, what would it be?"

Again, he paused and assumed a very lawyerlike stance. "I think you can probably guess what that deduction is. Can't you, Miranda? You've made a deduction, haven't you?"

"Yes," I said softly.

"And what is that?"

"Well, I know that anything is possible. A stranger in the shape of the man in brown may have slipped in and done it. But what I really think is, the person who murdered Sam Roberts was no outsider. It was someone who belonged to Jacob's Corner. But it wasn't my father, that I know."

So we agreed on something. No dissent showed in his face. "Beyond that, I think it was a tricky, complex thing. The police are used to crude violence. Anything else isn't their meat. But it's certainly something else we have here," he said.

I found myself hanging on to his words.

"There are some things you've got to remember, though, Miranda. One is that it must have been a highly personal reason for which the person committed the act. There never was any maniac on the loose. No one else stands in danger. That is, unless they snoop around and get too close to the truth. I think you ought to visit with your granddad, think placid and pleasant thoughts …and let the dead bury the dead."

What a ghoulish ring there was to that old line. I envisioned a conclave of ghosts. And the admonition rang true enough to strike me with a shudder or two, too. Still, I persisted. "People will always think Dad may have done it if the real murderer isn't found."

"Better that than…*other things.* Take my advice—it's free for you. Don't dig, Miranda. Roberts wasn't that much of a loss."

"That's a popular sentiment, your last thought."

We wandered under the huge old sycamore in front and spoke of more pleasant matters—what we'd been doing with our lives over the past six years. He told me about his position with a local law firm where he'd worked summers while in law school. He told me about his small apartment and an old house farther down the river that he hoped would come up for sale someday when he had the money to buy it.

The subject of old houses opened up a new line of conversation. I asked him, "Doug, do you know why this place is called Jacob's Corner?"

"I haven't the foggiest. Could be something commonplace, like it was the spot where Jacobs sold apples or squashes. Or it could be that Jacobs was hanged from one of the big trees around here by a lynch mob." He looked up. "Say, this would have been a dandy spot. Why? Some reason you want to know?"

"How morbid you are today. I was just wondering about the history of the house. Grandfather thinks it's about a hundred and fifty years old. Just imagine all the history it's seen."

"I'm sure it's a very old house. I don't know that much about such things. A search of old records could probably answer your question. Tom Garrity had some books on the history of the county. They're mine now. If you wanted to pore over them, you might learn something about your Jacobs or your house. I'd be happy to loan them to you."

"I'd appreciate that. I'd like to know something, and perhaps Grandfather would enjoy it. I was thinking of sketching the house and eventually doing a painting of it. It would be nice to know some history."

He nodded. "No telling what you might find out."

"Yes, that's true. Something horrendous might turn up. If it does, I may want to keep my mouth shut. If it's something worthy, I'll make it public. It'll give me something to do besides sketch while I'm here."

"Are you staying long?"

"I'm not sure. Grandfather asked me to stay a spell. I presume that means I'm welcome for a reasonable time. But who knows? I have a feeling Walter, Rita, and Leslie will stick like glue as long as I'm here. I may be headed for insanity shortly."

"I think I understand what you mean. Perhaps I can rescue you from them from time to time."

"Very well. If you hadn't volunteered, I might

have had to twist your arm." It was hard to believe
I was saying that to the once-obnoxious Doug
Lassiter.

I watched him drive away. Something told me
not to dwell on thoughts of Doug Lassiter. There
was enough going on in my life right now. But, oh,
how he had changed, and for the better.

The calico cat came padding along then and
rubbed vigorously against my ankles.

Aren't you the straightforward one? I thought.

But I couldn't get my mind off marionettes and
murder. There we had all been at lunchtime today.
All the prime suspects—there really was no other
way for me to look at it. And Doug had to be
included in the group.

CHAPTER VI

"Ah, romance."

Walter strolled up from behind me. I had just managed to keep from jerking at the unexpected voice. In thought, I had been far, faraway. "Don't be premature, Walter."

"You always were sweet on him, weren't you?" my uncle asked.

"Me? You've got to be kidding. I heartily disliked him. I went out of my way to avoid him. For your information, I have had a few little romances over the years. I haven't been sitting on the shelf all this time. But I haven't been swept off my feet yet. So don't let your imagination run away," I spluttered, surprising myself at my own foolish loquacity.

"I wouldn't think of it. But there is a fine line

between love and hate. If you're planning on an extended stay, who knows what might happen? Of course, you'd be wise not to fall for Lassiter. He's got his career on his mind. Wouldn't have much time for a woman. He's just starting out and has a long way to go."

"I never said I planned on an extensive stay. I didn't bring that much luggage with me." I should have told him to keep his nose out of my love life but decided I'd said quite enough already.

"It's probably just as well. It's boosted Dad's morale to see you, but I'm not so sure it's altogether a good idea, your visit. It's just reminded Dad of the past, of Richard, of the crime, of the trial, of Mama."

"I doubt that he needed me to be reminded of the past. Every time he goes to the den—"

Walter brushed my words away. He stroked his neat mustache and was silent for a few moments. What he said next more than surprised me. "Did you tell the truth, Miranda?"

The truth? At the trial?That was what he meant. A wave of anger mingled with shock convulsed me. Stonily, I stared at him. "You still think Dad did it," I muttered in disbelief, more to myself than to him.

He shrugged. "What else is there to think?"

"Do you think Leslie was lying, too? She'd at least have seen him come out of the room, according to the police theory, and might have seen him go in."

I knew before these words had been spoken that they held little water. We were talking about blood relatives. I knew as well as he that Leslie wouldn't have spoken the brutal truth and sent her brother to prison—either one of them.

"Did you ever ask Leslie if she was telling the truth?" I asked. "There are others who could have done it."

Walter was thoughtful. "Just because Leslie didn't see him go in or out the door is no proof he didn't do it."

"It adds to the weight of evidence in Dad's favor. Leslie knows he was out by the toolshed with me after Roberts arrived at the house. She walked away and left us out there."

"Leslie didn't see anyone go in or out the door, my dear. But the facts are that somebody did it."

"Most of the people here could have done it," I countered.

"Now that's interesting. Tell me how I could have done it."

I shook my head. "I don't think—"

"Come on. Be a sport. I'm not asking you to perjure yourself or jump out of a ten-story window. Just tell me how I could have done it."

"All right, Walter. If you insist. I won't be a stick-in-the-mud." I pondered, looking into his mildly inquisitive eyes. "Maybe you knew Sam Roberts was coming to the house at that time. You hid in the den and waited for him, behind the sofa perhaps."

"Then I must have been in collusion with Leslie, or was clairvoyant. How could I know she'd put him in the den and Richard would conveniently take his sweet time in seeing the man?"

"Thomas Garrity and Doug had already arrived and were ensconced in the living room. That left the den as a logical place to put another caller. A simple deduction. And it needn't have taken very long. Whoever did it had to have some luck on his side. Luck was something he couldn't count on. Things just went his way. Another possibility— from the upstairs window you saw the man arrive and simply went down the stairs and slipped into the den without being seen."

"With three people in view of the stairs from the living room, and Leslie in view of the door?" he asked skeptically.

"Doug went into the kitchen at one point. During that time Grandmother and Reverend Garrity had their backs to the living room doorway, at least for a short time. Nina went upstairs to do some cleaning, and they didn't see her. Ergo, Walter, if they missed Nina, they could have missed you. Anyway, they were all looking at snapshots. Their attention wasn't on the stairway. As for Leslie, even if she'd seen something—" I didn't finish. I knew he'd get the drift.

"So you're saying the others were distracted and didn't see me, and if Leslie saw me, she would have lied for me. Why so?"

"*Why so?* You know perfectly well, Walter. For a very elementary reason. Because blood is thicker than water. Leslie wouldn't send you to prison. She'd lie for you."

Walter rubbed his chin and gave me a squinty-eyed look. "And what about you,

Miranda? Do the rules of basic human behavior not apply to you? You would tell the truth and send your father to prison?"

My mouth flew open. I licked my lips. I shouldn't have let myself fall into Walter's trap. I should have seen it coming. But I hadn't. "I—I didn't face that dilemma," I stammered. "I was telling the truth. I wasn't forced to make a choice."

He stood arms akimbo and stared at the sky. "Your theory calls for a lot of tripping upstairs and downstairs, and not a soul noticing. Once for Nina and once or twice for me, depending on which version you favor. I don't know, Miranda. It's shaky, very shaky. How did I get out of the room, by the way? Why the malarkey about the letter opener in the woodwork? Why didn't I just walk out the door? You've already said Leslie wouldn't tell on me, and she was the only one who could see from where she was at."

"At the time you couldn't have known she was the only one who could see the door. You must have gone out one of the windows, probably the one at front. I recall the window exit as a minor theory the police toyed with. You could see there was no one around and slipped quickly out."

"And went back in and slipped up the stairs without being spotted. Then how did the window get locked? I came from upstairs after the body was found and Doug had checked the windows. I couldn't have done it, and neither could Rita—she was sleeping in the shade."

I chewed my lower lip. It was true enough. Even

accepting the risky theory that he'd sneaked up the stairs without being spotted, there was the matter of the window locked from inside.

"The only answer can be that someone in the room sneaked over during the excitement and locked the window," I said. "Someone in the family feared someone else in the family had done the deed. They noticed the one window was unlocked and sought to create the locked-room effect to throw off the police. You were the beneficiary of some unexpected assistance."

"That's pretty weak, Miranda. If someone did do that, they couldn't have been very bright. It would have been smarter to just leave the window unlocked, indicating the possibility of an outsider coming in and getting away."

He shook his head. "All this elaborate scheming, climbing out windows, is not my style. You know what I'd have done if I had killed the man, Miranda? I'd have walked out of the room, bold as brass, and shut the door. Then seeing that Leslie could see me but the others couldn't, I'd have walked right out the front door, probably gone out to where Rita was. I'd have brazened it out all the way. I hadn't threatened the man's life, and I wouldn't have worried about Leslie talking."

He wasn't finished. "Even if I managed the deed, I didn't have a motive. Motive, that's the thing. The prosecution doesn't have to prove motive, but they won't get too far in a case without one. Why would I have killed Sam Roberts?"

My eyes narrowed. I mulled it over. "I don't know," I said. "Why did you, Walter?" I really hadn't meant to sound quite so accusatory.

He was taken aback. Then he gave out a series of nervous, throaty little laughs. "Why, Miranda. I think you suspect I was the one. Don't be foolish. You know I couldn't do anything like that. Why, I couldn't crack a fish over the head, let alone a human being."

Maybe he couldn't, and maybe he could, was all I could tell myself.

"Anyway," he continued, "why bother yourself? Richard was acquitted. He can't be tried again. Double jeopardy, you know."

"Yes, I know about double jeopardy. But you know about human nature. Some people will always think Dad was guilty."

Walter made a production of stooping to stroke the cat, to indicate his gentleness, I supposed.

But his next words certainly lacked the milk of human kindness. "Sam Roberts deserved what he got. The world is better off without him. Who really cares?"

That was a very popular sentiment, I had discovered.

He went on. "If that prosecutor hadn't been all gung ho and tried to get Rich on murder one, the jury might have handed him a guilty verdict. As it was, they didn't buy it, either, that killing a no-account like Roberts should get someone life in the pen."

I'd preferred to think the jury had searched and found the truth, but what my uncle said was a possibility, I had to admit.

"I believed in Sam Roberts, I admit it," he said.

"I believed in him the day he was killed. It wasn't until later that I learned you couldn't trust him any farther than you could throw him."

I broke off the rather unpleasant conversation and went into the kitchen for a cool drink. I needed it.

Nina was making an apple pie and looked up from the floured board to see who had come in. "Oh, it's you, Miranda. Nice boy, that Doug Lassiter."

"Yes, seems to be. He's changed a lot."

"Smart, too. Getting through law school and passing that bar examination is real rough."

"Takes a lot of grit and determination, I'd expect."

"I guess lots of things take that, though. It is good the way he comes to see your grandfather. There's nothing to make him do it. I like to see a young person show some consideration of older folks. Some wouldn't bother."

I hoped she wasn't making a pointed remark for my benefit.

"Of course, I'm not talking about you," she added hastily and seemed a little embarrassed. "That's different—entirely different." She said no more about it then. I suspected she thought she had overstepped her bounds.

I turned to a safer subject. "Ummm...apple pie for dinner. I probably won't want to leave if you cook like this all the time."

"I didn't think my cooking was anything special, just the same old six and seven, it seems like to me. You probably have a lot to get back to, I suppose."

"Nothing pressing. I don't think it would look good if I whisked down and whisked back. Anyway, I have a project planned for here. It will take a little time."

The crust tore when she picked it up, and she scolded herself.

I mused that even experienced cooks have trouble with piecrust.

I went up to my room then and plopped down in the rocking chair to think things over.

The conversation with Walter was still fresh in my mind. Even though he had toppled or weakened by derision each theory I had advanced, I had no intention of eliminating him from my list of suspects. A good detective would take nothing for granted. I'd read enough murder mysteries to know that.

So now I was a detective. Why not?

I knew I should not overlook anyone present that day if I was to be perfectly objective. But on the other hand, my personal acquaintance with all involved subjects gave me an insight into those candidates most unlikely.

Grandmother and the Reverend Garrity could be eliminated. Both were pious and God-fearing, as well as in frail health, and they were together the entire time. In addition, I knew my father should not be considered a suspect. Doug Lassiter, as a possibility, was pretty weak, as he had left the living room only briefly for a drink from the kitchen. But he was still a possibility.

And none of the others should be excluded, even in the absence of a motive.

There was Leslie, for example. Some of her testimony could not be corroborated by any other witness. There was only her word that the man had arrived while she was out front, that she showed him to the den and left the door partly open.

Conceivably, she could have followed the man into the den, shut the door behind her, and struck him down while he was off his guard. Then she could have jammed the letter opener into the crack behind the door facing, climbed out a front window, and casually come back in. Doug had testified that he believed the door to the den was shut when he came back from the kitchen. So it would have fit in. Of course, Doug might have lied. But why?

It sounded preposterous. But someone had struck the man down and quickly escaped from the room. There was no gainsaying that.

Leslie had never shown a propensity for violence, but she was capable of blustering through it all, just as Walter had averred he would do. And she had the opportunity of whisking over and locking the window during the excitement following the finding of the body. All innocent eyes would have been glued mainly on the motionless body, not watching what everyone else was doing.

But I drew a blank trying to come up with a plausible motive. After Dad had lambasted Walter, she had sympathized with him. Yet in some ways she had better sense than her younger brother and must have suspected Roberts might be up to no good. Even so, it hardly seemed a strong enough reason to commit murder.

I told myself I ought not to put the cart before the horse. Whoever did the killing had a motive. It was as simple as that.

Suddenly I felt as if I were in a maelstrom, smack in the middle of whirling events I did not understand. For the time being, I put an end to speculations and attempted deductions.

CHAPTER VII

We partook of a reasonably quiet Saturday supper.

A little later I was alone in the living room, looking at a magazine, and Rita sidled up to me with something obviously on her mind.

"Why didn't you get Dougie to take you out, it being Saturday night and all?" she asked.

"I'm not that forward, Rita."

"You could have thrown a hint or two."

"What makes you think I wanted to go out?" I asked.

"Aha! Now you're pretending. You were always fond of him, weren't you? You only acted like you didn't like him. That's what everyone thought."

"I really didn't like him, Rita. I thought he was obnoxious."

"Oh, well, that was years ago. He's darned good-looking and has a bright future now. He'd make a good catch."

I shrugged.

"Walter says you've had some broken romances."

"What girl hasn't? They were minor episodes, about one candle power."

"Maybe you'd like to talk about them."

"I really don't think so. They were nothing traumatic. I guess I'm just choosy."

"I've had a lot of experience along those lines. I might be able to offer some advice."

I had no expectation at all of profiting from her advice. But I said, growing a little weary of the conversation, "It's no big deal. I've been attracted to a couple of fellows. Each time something turned up to turn me off."

"I know. Like finding out he's insanely jealous, or blows every dime he makes on cars or stereo equipment, or you can't trust him with your best friend."

"And they say women come in infinite variety," I said.

Rita nodded her curly head in agreement. "Men can be such rotters. Just the same—" She paused and seemed to lose the thread of her thought. "How long are you planning to stay, anyway?"

"I'm really not sure." I'd already told her that once.

This time she tossed her curly head. "Why did you really come here?"

"Why, I came because Grandfather asked me to come. Perhaps pleaded is a better word."

She cocked her head to the left and touched an enameled fingertip to her temple. "I know I shouldn't be nosy, but—well, did your grandfather ask Richard to come, too?"

"I don't think so, but frankly I wouldn't be surprised if that were to come about in the future. I really can't say what's in Grandfather's mind or Dad's."

"It's just odd, you turning up all of a sudden." She lowered her voice then. "You—you're not here to do a little bit of detecting, are you? Do you have some new ideas on the murder? Walter says you practically accused him of doing it. Why, you must know that's preposterous. You're way off base."

"I did not come here to try to solve the murder. If that were the outcome, I would not object. But it's all just as muddled as it was that day."

I thought there was relief on her face, but I could have been mistaken.

"I've always felt there was a clue somewhere that everybody has overlooked," she said. "Probably, it's something that is staring all of us in the face. Don't you agree, Miranda?"

"Yes, I've thought so myself."

"You've been trying to figure out ways that everyone could have done it, haven't you?"

"I guess I always have done that. I'm just naturally curious. I can't help myself."

She straightened up and took a deep breath. "You've done Walter. Now you must do me."

"Do you?"

"Yes, tell me how I could have committed the crime. I am a suspect the same as everyone else."

"Don't you think this is something better left undone?"

"No. I am a suspect. I demand the chance to defend myself."

"Rita, I just don't think—you haven't been asked to defend yourself."

Rita was adamant. "I really do insist."

I still didn't like it but reluctantly agreed in order to placate Rita.

"Well," I began, "there is no one to corroborate your whereabouts all during the critical period. You said you were on the east side of the house, reading and then sleeping in the shade. You might have seen the man go in with Leslie. It wouldn't have been too difficult to escape detection. One of the windows held an air conditioner. The others were somewhat opaque with both sheers and draperies. Until Leslie joined the group with refreshments, there was no one seated in view of the door to the den. You could have simply slipped into the den and struck the man down—for reasons known only to you. Perhaps you were afraid Walter was getting involved in a shady deal and Sam Roberts wouldn't listen to reason."

"Well, honey, I've known men who wouldn't listen to reason before, but I've never cold-cocked one. How could I have done it? I'm not very muscular. Wouldn't the man have fought back?"

"He was struck from behind, remember. He

turned his back on someone, making it perhaps more likely that it was a woman, someone he would not fear. If he had been afraid, surely he would have called out for help. Someone would have heard that over the sounds of the air conditioner."

She shook her head almost disdainfully. "And I got out of the room by what means?"

"The window is the only way I can figure out."

"So I climbed out one of the front windows and sneaked back around the house. Why didn't I just go out the door and out the front?"

"You must have sneaked a peek and saw Leslie sitting there in view of the door. You had to get out some other way."

"Then how did the window get locked? I was nowhere near that room when the body was discovered and the place checked."

It always came back to the locked window. I sighed. "I really don't know, but someone in the family must have locked it. They must have had the idea the locked-room bit would add a stupefying factor to the crime, making it virtually unsolvable. You benefited from a chance act, if you can call it benefited. In retrospect it seems a foolish thing to have done. Much better to have left the window unlocked, indicating anyone could have come in from the outside and escaped undetected."

"So, assuming I did it, I sneaked around the house and casually snoozed off in a lawn chair."

"You needn't have been asleep."

"But I was. And some murderer maybe walking right near me. If I'd waked and seen—well, I'd probably be pushing up daisies myself."

"Now, fair is fair," I said. "Why don't you tell me your version of what might have happened."

"All right, I will. The man in brown. I think he was the one who did it. Probably someone Roberts had defrauded. Walter or I wouldn't have had any reason to harm Roberts at that time. Of course, we wouldn't resort to violence even if we had a reason. Anyway, it was later when Walter found out Roberts really was a con man. I think someone was following Roberts, sneaked in and did the dirty work, and climbed out the window and got away."

"And how did the window get locked?" I asked.

"Probably the way you said. Someone thinking they would get someone in the family off the hook by creating the locked-door effect."

"If someone—the man in brown—wanted to do Roberts in, why didn't he do it in a secluded spot?"

"Oh, somebody's house is much better. Throws the police completely off. This house was ideal because your father had threatened the man. I read a mystery once where a body was left in someone's library to throw the police off."

At least her theory excluded my father. "I see your point, but our elusive man in brown was taking a whale of a risk, what with it being broad daylight and people all around."

"People will take risks when they're desperate enough, or angry enough. It worked, didn't it?"

"But why the letter opener in the door?"

"Oh, that's simple," Rita said.

I waited with fascination.

"So nobody could come in while he was wiping off fingerprints from the poker and maybe other places, and getting out the window. He could see out the windows that there was nobody nearby. He figured he could sneak out the front and get away, and he did. Then some idiot locked the window trying to be helpful."

Sometimes a child comes up with a sage observation. I felt that such a thing had happened here. Rita's intellect had never impressed me. In fact, I considered her bordering on the simple-minded. Although that is probably too harsh. She was simply of average intelligence, with limited interests. Yet she had said something just now that struck me as being very perceptive.

For some reason I had always considered the letter opener in the facing an artful effect designed to help create the locked-room setting. Now I thought that Rita might be absolutely correct. The opener barred the door to momentarily keep others out, not to create illusions.

"Roberts wasn't a good man, anyway," Rita went on. "It may sound mean, but—well, someone did the world a good turn." There was a cold gleam in her eyes, I noticed.

I was disgusted that I had let myself be goaded once again into such an unpleasant conversation. I made up my mind I was not going through such a thing with any of the others. Still, the conversation with Rita was on my mind.

Rita's theory made as much sense as the others.

It did explain Nina's stubborn insistence she had seen what appeared to be a man in brown through the sidelights by the front door. The man would have had to reap the unexpected benefit of a resident's having locked the window later—I always came back to that window.

Also, he had enjoyed all around good luck, not to have been spotted except for the one brief glimpse, which Nina had ignored at the time. She had not even recalled the incident until a second question session with a police officer. Somehow, the man in brown had to figure.

Rita had fitted him neatly into her theory. Fitting him into any of mine was like trying to force the wrong puzzle pieces together. The man in brown surely would have been a man Roberts trusted. Roberts had turned his back on him.

I went out into the hall to look at the sidelights. They were composed of thick, wavy old glass and were narrow insets to begin with. It was nearly dark now, but I had a feeling Nina's view would not have been a clear one. *The man in brown.* I touched a finger to the old glass.

The feeling came to me that I was being watched. I turned and saw no one. Then I went up the stairs to my little room.

Thoughts of murder and the man in brown still preoccupied my mind. I couldn't quite go along with Rita. I had decided, and Doug had agreed with me, that the murder was done by someone at Jacob's Corner. We thought it was a spur-of-the-moment act. Someone saw an opportunity and took it, and luck was with him. There had to be a genuine motive. And somewhere in all of that figured a man in brown. It was a fact I could not ignore.

When I turned out the light in my room that night, a fat moon sent lambent rays through the window. How peaceful the room seemed, washed with moonglow.

I wondered if I would ever be totally at peace.

Or would I spend the rest of my life seeing visions of little marionettes moving around— going upstairs and down, shutting doors, locking windows—in uncertain patterns through a shroud of mist?

CHAPTER VIII

Sunday morning found the daily routine changed slightly. Grandfather had his early breakfast and took the Sunday magazine outside to peruse in the warm sunshine. By ten the rest of us, sluggards all, had risen and were preparing to sit down in the kitchen to our morning meal. The food looked good and the room was filled with tempting aromas.

The promise of a pleasant repast, however, was quickly dulled.

We had seated ourselves, and Nina had gone to the refrigerator for a little tray of assorted jellies and jams. As she approached the table, in her usual calm manner, Rita spoke up brightly. "Tell Nina how she committed the murder, Miranda."

Nina looked stricken, as if she had heard a voice from the heavens call down to her. The jelly jars clattered and came close to tumbling out of the tray.

Walter snapped, "For Pete's sake, Rita, what's the matter with you?"

Rita looked stricken herself. "I wasjustjoking. I didn't mean it, Nina. It's just that Miranda's playing detective and figuring out ways everyone who was here that day could have done the murder. She's done Walter and me. I was just making a little joke."

Hard lines had formed between Nina's pale eyes. She scowled, then set the jelly tray down. "Some things shouldn't be joked about," she solemnly intoned and went out of the room.

"Don't go making Nina sore," Walter said testily to his wife. He spoke softly, but a sibilant undertone was harsh. "Have you ever thought about what we'd do if she quit? Dad needs somebody here, and Nina is dependable. She keeps the house clean, the meals cooked, and gets along with the old man. You know how high-handed Dad can be. Some women wouldn't take it."

"I'm sure we'd find someone else," Rita said halfheartedly.

"Don't count on it," he snapped.

Walter had a personal stake in the matter. Rita should have understood it as well as anyone else. Lack of a housekeeper would be a problem for Grandfather, and it would be one that would fall to Leslie and Walter. Heaven forbid that *he* should have to turn a hand around the place! And Nina's pies and hot biscuits were not necessary for life, but they were a delight worth preserving.

Leslie remained very cool, studying everyone and casually rubbing one of her earlobes. "He's right. We don't want to antagonize Nina. What a dreadful thing to say. I don't know how you can be facetious so early in the morning, Rita."

"I wish you wouldn't use words I don't know the meaning of," Rita replied.

Leslie's retort was milder than I expected. "I'm afraid I don't know what words other people do or do not know." She made rather a production of stirring some sweetener into her coffee and taking a lingering sip. "You must explain how I could have done the murder," she said to me. "I had so many opportunities and I might have wanted to protect Walter or something."

No way, I told myself. Not again. "Perhaps some other time."

"Yes," Walter said. "I'm tired of hearing about murder—murder, murder, murder. I don't see why it can't be forgotten."

Rita, of course, would dog the subject. "We've all tried to figure out how everyone else could have done it. I have. Haven't you, Leslie?"

Leslie remained cool. She laid down the fork in her hand and put her elbows on the table, interlacing her fingers as a resting place for her chin. "Yes—oh, so many times."

"I know what we should do," Rita said, clapping her hands together. "We should all figure out how...*Miranda could have done it.*"

Rita had scored her Brownie points. They were all regaled.

I was far from regaled. I was tempted to impale them all with an icy stare and murmur with an acid tone, as Queen Victoria was rumored to have done: "We are not amused."

But all I did was smile weakly. And I endeavored to keep my mouth shut during the rest of the meal. Surrounded by Calvins, it was the safer course.

I had begun to wonder if I had been wrong to come back to Jacob's Corner.

My only purpose had been to see an old man whom I had not seen for many years. If he wanted to make peace with me and my parents, I wanted to give him the chance. That was all.

I had found it impossible, however, to return to the house and associate with the people involved in the earlier incident without feeling a resurging desire to know the truth. In addition, I didn't think I was a welcome guest in the eyes of some people here. Everyone was anxious to know when I was going home. I seemed to pose a threat to them all.

I'd have to think things over. Creating further acrimony among the people at Jacob's Corner had not been my goal. And if my deduction was correct that someone here had done the killing, it might not even be safe for me to stay.

After breakfast, I escaped with my sketchbook and found a shaded spot at the verge of the cornfield across the road, giving me a clear view of the front of Jacob's Corner.

To clear from my mind the thoughts of little

marionettes running about, I dwelled upon the area's history and the place that Jacob's Corner might have played in it.

Tracing the double chimneys, the wide eaves, the facade of brick, I could not help wondering about the hands that had done the work, laid the bricks, and hammered the nails. What sort of things had gone on during the years the house had stood? Had there been other tragedies? Had others died within the walls? So much must have happened, and so little was known.

But the brick house stood silent. It had kept its secrets very well.

After lunch, I continued to sketch. I was finding it difficult to concentrate and was not satisfied with the work I was doing.

Then I was interrupted by the appearance of Doug Lassiter, not a disagreeable interruption—he had changed so much. He parked his car just off the road and came toward me.

"Oh, you are good," he said, sitting down beside me on the short log I occupied.

I smiled. "Fair," I told him. "I've got a long way to go."

"Don't we all?" The half grin showed. "How's everything at Jacob's cozy Corner today?"

I gave him a lopsided scowl. "About the usual—that's why I've run away."

"Was it that bad?"

"Maybe. Did you ever get the feeling you weren't wanted?" I could have bitten my tongue. It had been an unfortunate choice of words. As a child Doug had been unwanted and deprived, and hadn't had a decent life at all until the Garritys took him in.

But he was nonchalant. "All the time."

"I'm beginning to wonder if I should have stayed home."

"Somebody giving you a hard time?" he asked.

"The whole Calvin family is a pain." I went on to tell him about Rita's breakfast bombshell and a few other things.

"Just like Rita to do something like that. I'll bet Nina was steaming."

"No. She was glacial."

Doug was thoughtful. Then he rose, his hands in his pockets, and surveyed the heavens. He was very lawyerlike now and looked as if he might be ready to present his summary to the jury. He said, "Reckon you'd better do me."

I was simply horrified. Yet deep down I had to admit he still *was* one of my suspects.

He was smiling, white teeth showing.

"I'm no longer *doing* people," I said.

"Why, I think you're serious. Sorry about that. I was just trying my hand at a little humor. You've forgotten my little bit of advice, haven't you?"

My eyes met his in a swift glance.

"About not digging, I mean."

"I didn't mean to be blatant about it," I said softly. "But Walter egged me on, got me to say things. Then he told it all to Rita and I got the third degree from her. Sometimes things seem to snowball. But I'm being good as gold now. I'm trying to keep a distance between myself and the rest of them. I wish they'd all go home...and of course they wish the same thing about me."

"Just one big happy family. Say, I've dug out two old books, histories of the area. Maybe they'll give you something to do for a while."

"I appreciate that. I really do."

"I always try to ingratiate myself with beautiful women."

I should have sloughed off the comment, but I didn't quite. It struck a chord of awareness in me that I tried to hide with a chuckle. There was something about him...something that defied sloughing off.

"It's odd, isn't it?" he said. "You and I after several years, I mean. Neither of us married or anything. You haven't got anything going, have you?"

"Noooo—not at the moment."

"Good. I'm pretty busy most of the time, but I thought I could get away tomorrow night. There's a summer theater not too far from here. I thought you might enjoy seeing a play. I've heard it's pretty good, if your taste runs to that sort of thing. It's a modern dress version of *Hamlet.*"

I nodded. "I think I might enjoy that."

"I'll be by about seven then. Right now I've got to run along. Sorry I can't hang around, but I've got a lot of reading to do."

I walked with him to his car, where he handed me the two books, gave me his quick half grin, and drove away.

Anxious to have a look at the books, I picked up

my art materials and walked up the drive and over to the front door. My arms were full and it was all I could do to turn the knob and push the front door open.

Leslie saw my plight and came to shut the door. "You look busy as a little beaver. Why didn't Doug come in?"

"He has homework."

"Yes, a lawyer would." She eyed the books but didn't comment.

Nina came through the hall, smiled at me, and glanced at my load in silence.

I slipped up to my little room for a closer look at the books Doug had brought me.

One book had first been printed before the turn of the century. Foxed and ragged about the edges, it hadn't borne its years with exceptional grace. But it seemed an interesting treatise concerned with life along the Ohio River for the past two centuries.

The second volume was somewhat slimmer. It had first been printed in 1910 and was limited to the history of the county in which Grandfather resided.

I looked through both books in a cursory fashion for an hour or more.

A little later I moseyed downstairs and found Nina preparing chicken salad for our Sunday night supper. I poured a small glass of lemonade and hopped up on a kitchen stool near her.

"You're keeping mighty busy, drawing and studying and all," she said to me.

"It's best to keep busy around here," I said. "I hope to complete a painting of the house later on. It'll be after I return home. I won't have the time now."

"Not leaving already, are you?"

"Oh, no, not for a while, I'm sorry to say."

She rubbed the end of her ample nose. "Why, what would you be sorry for?"

I took a sip of lemonade. "Just that as long as I'm around the others will probably be around, too. It makes extra cooking and work for you."

"I don't mind that. It's my job to do those things. Of course, there are certain people I wouldn't mind to see leave." Her chin jutted out, as if she did mean business.

"I don't think I'd let Rita upset me if I were you. Putting her foot in her mouth is what she does best," I said.

Nina snorted. "The very idea," she muttered.

I shook my head in agreement. "She's a card, that Rita."

"It was a sad day when that man Sam Roberts came to this home," Nina said.

That was the truth if ever it had been spoken, I thought. But I'd never discussed the killing with Nina and was surprised that she brought up the subject.

"He was a bad man and all he brought this house was misery," she went on.

"Everyone seems agreed on that point, Nina. He wasn't a good man." There were myriad questions I wanted to ask her, but I debated the propriety of such a course. At length, I waded in. "It's a shame you didn't get a better look at that other man, Nina. The man in brown."

She studied the stalk of celery in her hand. "Yes. I just couldn't see him no better. And then that prosecutor making out like it was all a lie."

Somehow she seemed aggrieved, and I decided it was prudent to change subjects. "Did your great-grandmother ever say anything about this house, Nina?"

Her lips pursed. "It was a long time ago and I was just a wee sprout when she was alive in her old age."

"Of course. But surely somebody knows something about this house."

"It's not like it once was," she told me. "People move around and lots of things get lost in the shuffle. I'd venture that most people around here couldn't tell you what went on twenty-five years ago, let alone a hundred forty years ago."

She was right. But it would be nice if some old old-timer filled with knowledge of the past appeared to talk to me. I knew that wasn't likely to happen, so I'd have to put much stock in two musty old books.

At supper Grandfather, whom I hadn't seen too much of that day, got straight to the point. "What kind of mysterious activities are you up to, girl? What were you carrying an armful of books up to your room for?" He was wrapped up in a cardigan sweater again.

I saw nothing mysterious about having two

books under my arm. Inwardly I heaved a sigh. Nothing I did seemed to escape the attention of all the others, and the grapevine worked like a charm.

I told him, "Nothing mysterious, Grandfather. Just some old history books Doug thought I might find interesting."

"It sounds dull to me," Rita said. "I never did like history…or math…or English."

"You never know when something interesting might turn up," I said.

"Looking for something in particular?" Leslie asked. She had her calculating look on, but that wasn't unusual.

"No. I just thought it would be interesting to know what life was like around here in earlier days. This house is pretty old. Maybe I'll even find out something about it and some of the people who lived here."

"If it does predate the Civil War, I'm sure it has seen a lot of excitement," Leslie said. "It would be interesting to know. Perhaps the house is a historical landmark. Wouldn't that be nice, Daddy? You could put up a little sign designating the house as such."

"I sure don't know what would be nice about it," Grandfather said. "It would just attract a lot of fool tourists to drive by and stare."

"Now, Daddy. Supposing General Grant spent the night here, or accepted the surrender of an opposing Confederate officer. That would be something to brag about."

Slowly buttering his biscuit, Grandfather was

thoughtful. "Why not have President Lincoln reading the Emancipation Proclamation from the front steps?"

"That's ridiculous," Rita said. "He called his cabinet together in Washington, D.C. to read it."

A shocked hush came over all of us.

"How did *you* know that?" Leslie demanded, her green eyes narrowed almost to slits.

"Oh, I read it in the newspaper one day. You know those little fillers they put in when they have some space and nothing to go there."

Rita could be full of surprises, but we all agreed we sometimes read those little tidbits of information.

After dinner, I finished a long letter I'd started to my parents. Then I returned to a perusal of the history books.

CHAPTER IX

On Monday morning I dashed out to the mailbox with the letter. The red flag was up, so I knew someone else had deposited mail already and that the postman hadn't yet come.

The letter already inside the box caught my eye. It was addressed to someone I knew very well—my own father. And the unsteady handwriting could belong to no one but my grandfather.

I deposited my letter and slowly closed the little door. Now I certainly had some food for thought.

The rest of the day I parceled my time among three basic activities—sketching, reading, and pondering the contents of Grandfather's missive to my father. After lunch, I devoted my attention to the history of the local county. A careful reading seemed in order.

A chapter that commanded my interest concerned the abolitionist cause of pre-Civil War days. I was fascinated by the chronicles of exploits of members of the bedrock opposition to slavery.

The author had warmed up to his subject and was beginning to discuss the foremost individuals in the cause and their contributions to it. I turned a page and the next line did not seem to have any connection with the sentence on the previous page. A quick check of the page numbers told me why. A page was missing.

My lips drew into an involuntary moue. Why did it have to be that particular page? How I detested people who mutilated books! Although what I had read was interesting, the material on the missing page seemed even more interesting.

Reading beyond the missing page, I learned of a trial in the 1840s. A slave, having lived temporarily in free territory after being brought there by a careless master, petitioned for his freedom. In this case, the slave had won his freedom. It seemed similar to me to the Dred Scott case later, which had gone the other way and had further shattered the already precarious relationship between North and South.

I made it a point to question Doug about the page just as soon as we were on our way to the theater that evening.

"No, I didn't know there was a page missing," he told me. "But it wouldn't surprise me. They're old books. Don't worry about it. Most books of that vintage aren't valuable, I don't think."

"The book was interesting, and the devil of it is, I was particularly interested in the section where the page was missing."

"You don't think a page would be missing from a section you weren't interested in, do you?" he teased.

I gave him a languid sidelong glance. "No. Things don't work that way, do they?"

"Not on your life. What was so interesting, anyway?"

"A chapter on the abolition cause. It discussed the roles of various people and the contributions they made in fighting slavery."

"I see." He mused in silence for a time, then spoke. "This area was probably a hotbed of abolitionist activities, since it bordered a slave state just across the river."

"It would have been a major thoroughfare for escaping slaves, wouldn't it?" I asked.

"It sure would. Escaping from Kentucky or Virginia was a heck of a lot easier than escaping from the Deep South."

"The river looks so wide and menacing for someone to try to cross, someone on the run who had no boat," I said.

"Where there's a will, there's a way. Anyway, there were people all along who helped, remember. When a slave made it to someone friendly, that person led him to someone else who was friendly, and so it went."

"Yes, and a lot of them did make successful runs, didn't they?" I couldn't help shuddering, thinking about the ones who didn't make it safely.

"You look grim, Miranda. It's not all that becoming."

"I was thinking grim thoughts. It's a habit with me, I'm afraid."

"We'll have to do something about that."

I turned to look at him and saw that he had turned to look at me. He was smiling in the way I remembered him doing so well. Yet there was something very different in his eyes. I pointed at the windshield. "The road is that way," I said pleasantly. "The ditch doesn't look too accommodating."

He turned his eyes back to the road without protest. "You know, I've often wondered over the past several years how you turned out."

"Hmmm...that makes me sound like a new recipe for lemon meringue pie. But, seriously, I suppose people always feel that way when they've been involved in a murder together."

He scowled. "You always get back to that, don't you?"

"Yes, it may not be healthful, but after all, my father was the only one charged with the crime."

"Perhaps that in part is why I've thought about you over the years, not only wondering about the crime, but how you held together. You showed a lot of fortitude in the face of the hammering the prosecutor gave you."

"It was a grueling experience in the fullest sense of the word. But, of course, I was telling the truth. If I'd been lying, he'd have made mincemeat of me.

"It wouldn't have been the first time a prosecutor made mincemeat of someone who was telling the truth. There are ways—"

"That sounds frightening, as if it's a game, and to the victor goes the spoils. Is the same man still prosecutor?"

"Umm…hmmm. Wilkinson. He still goes at it pretty good, but he's lost some of the drive of his earliest days."

"I'll bet he's never forgotten your smart-mouth answer on the witness stand. *Why I thought that thump was someone being murdered in Mr. Calvin's den, Mr. Prosecutor.*"

"Don't rub it in. I'm still trying to live that one down."

A feeling of smugness had crept over me. "Wilkinson lost his first big case—he never broke me," I said.

Doug laughed. "Now you're frightening me. You sound like one of those women in the old movies you see late at night on TV—gutsy and all that."

"I'm a Calvin. I get it honestly. It's not our way to be meek and mild." I was thoughtful. "He never broke any of us."

Doug gave me a cool lawyer look. I expected something erudite to come from his lips. He said, "Just don't get too big for your britches."

I giggled. "That's what my father used to tell me. You sound just like my father, Doug."

"Not by design," he said. "But I do mean it. You're still determined to find out who did Sam Roberts in, aren't you?"

"*Who did Sam Roberts in?* Sounds like the title of a murder mystery. I didn't come here for that purpose. It's just now that I'm here, all I see are reminders and I can't keep the little marion—I can't keep thoughts about that day out of my mind. Someone did it and there's got to be a clue someplace that's been overlooked."

"I'm afraid you've read too many of those murder mysteries where the fabled sleuth is called in years after the crime has taken place and digs up the facts, takes statements, and abracadabra solves the murder. Real life is different, Miranda."

"You're too young to sound so staid. You ought to be helping me. We could team up and put our brains together."

"I've told you before—if you persist, someone is going to get jittery. And then, who knows what might happen?"

"I've begun to keep a low profile, as they say. Everyone thinks I'm concerned with my sketching and reading of old history books. Nothing harmful in those things."

"You are a stubborn one."

"Does that mean we aren't going to team up to solve the mystery?"

He sighed lightly, resignedly. "What do you want from me?"

"Your powers of logic. You must have pondered what happened. Surely you've had more opinions and ideas than you've told me so far."

"I've told you I thought it was someone at Jacob's Corner, didn't I? And that it was a complex crime."

"Yes, and we are in agreement."

"I think it was something unplanned. Someone saw their chance and took it, or was provoked and reacted instantly."

I mimicked applause. "We're thinking alike."

He continued. "The killer was successful, but not because of carefully laid plans. Do you follow me, Miranda? Coming up is the quintessence of my theories. The killer was successful because he—or she—succeeded."

I thought his words over. "They say that nothing succeeds like success. There is great truth in the saying."

"The problem is the locked window. It shouldn't have been locked, but it was, and therein lies the real mystery."

"So?"

"So it was impossible for the crime to have happened the way it seems, but it did happen, so it wasn't impossible. That's not very profound stuff to be coming from a lawyer, is it?"

"So it didn't happen the way it seems. That much makes sense. Why are you so sure?"

"About the window? Well, I checked the windows myself as soon as I realized what had happened. The windows were definitely locked. I testified that I didn't believe anyone had gone over and snapped on any lock between the time your dad pushed the door in and then. I wasn't standing guard over the windows, so it would have been presumptuous for me to assert *absolutely* that no window had been touched. But I am convinced in my mind that no one did touch them. As a kid, I may not have been perfect—I was an obnoxious cuss, wasn't I? I had my faults and my weaknesses, but without bragging, I would have to say that I had a remarkable faculty for observation. I say that no one walked across the room and touched any window."

"That is interesting, and it does change the whole picture."

"It surely does. Remember what the detective of Baker Street said. It was something to the effect that when the impossible has been eliminated, what is left, no matter how improbable, must be the truth. You say your dad was with you until just before he pushed in the door. I say the windows were already locked when he pushed in the door. There really are only three basic solutions."

I was ready to listen to all three of them.

"One—someone ingeniously figured out a way, from outside the room, to put the letter opener behind the facing or to lock the window. Now I'm not saying that couldn't be done. For some people it might be child's play. Magicians do the seemingly impossible, with a little or a whole heap of preparation. But on the spur of the moment the average person—"

"So we'll cross off that solution, unless we turn up a suspect who happens to be a magician," I said.

"Then we mustn't overlook the possibility of a secret way out of the room."

"Sliding panels and secret passages, etcetera, etcetera."

"The police were contemptuous of that theory," he continued. "But nevertheless the room was checked over. They didn't find any sliding panels. The ceiling and every floorboard were checked. That sort of thing is all very well if you live in a fifteenth-century castle in merrie old England, but here on the Ohio it doesn't, shall we say, hold much water."

"The third solution?"

Doug shrugged. "Roberts locked the window or stuck the letter opener behind the facing himself."

There must have been something of a wide-eyed look on my face.

"I know it doesn't make a lot of sense, but sometimes people don't die instantly of a blow such as he received."

"That's true enough," I admitted.

"If he had been dazed by the blow at first, he might have got to his feet after the assailant slipped out of the room, staggered around, and, thinking of self-preservation only, grabbed the letter opener and secured the door. There's no way to say it didn't happen that way. Fingerprints on the opener were not discernible."

"He secured the door, then fell over dead," I mused. "It sounds very much like something Shakespeare might have come up with. Some of his characters had such a penchant for dying perorations."

"A plague on both your houses. 'Tis not so deep as a well, nor as wide as a…churchyard?" He pondered a moment, then continued with his rather haphazard and amusing version of Mercutio's dying speech.

I politely applauded his efforts, then went on to

other matters. "It's something I don't think I've ever thought of before, that Roberts himself secured the door. It plays havoc with all my theories. Almost anyone could have done the crime with more ease than I had previously thought. The man in brown could have done it. He doesn't fit in with our lines of deduction, but he has to fit in somewhere." I sighed deeply. "So where does that leave us?"

"Almost at the theater," Doug said.

How quickly the miles had melted away. I had paid little attention to anything on the drive except our discussion about past history. Now the big red barn theater was just before us and it was time to focus on something else.

He pulled into the parking area. "The girl can't keep murder off her mind," he murmured. "And I had to take her to see *Hamlet.*"

We went to a steakhouse afterward, an ordinary, unpretentious place, but we didn't have too many choices.

We ordered. Then I was silent while mulling over the plot of the play we had just seen. "It would be so convenient," I said, "to have a play like Hamlet did. I'd work up a skit depicting the murder, make certain the culprit was there to see—"

Doug reached across the little square table and touched a finger to my lips, silencing them. "We've had enough of that tonight."

I took the chastisement meekly. "You're right. I'm beginning to sound like a broken record. I won't say another word about...about all that."

He gave me his half grin. We spent the rest of the evening talking about everything but murder.

It started to drizzle on the way home.

I didn't mind. The ground had become parched and dusty and the moisture was badly needed. In addition, it somehow seemed a soothing, finishing ending to the evening.

It was well after midnight when we returned to Grandfather's, but neither of us seemed anxious to put an end to the evening. We sat in the car in the dark, with the steady rain droning on around us. We talked quietly.

Soon the rain stopped and we went to the front door. Doug's arm was on my shoulder and I realized I was coming under his spell. Doug Lassiter, the nineteen-year-old who'd annoyed me, now affected me in a very different way. I couldn't help it, darn it. He wasn't like anyone else I'd ever known. So far no despicable trait or vexing habit had come to light. Far from it. He had traits I found highly desirable—kindness and thoughtfulness not the least of them.

But I was thankful he didn't start kissing me or pawing at me or anything of the sort just now.

I went in, put the chain on the door, turned out the hall light, and crept up the stairs to my room.

Despite the late hour, I wasn't sleepy. Lulled by the softly crooning pitter-patter at the window-panes—for the rain had started again—I plopped down in the rocker and turned introspective.

I thought about all the things Doug had said, and in particular about the three theories he had advanced. Each one seemed incredible. But if

Doug had been right and the windows were already locked when Dad broke in the door, one of the theories had to be correct, as improbable as it seemed. If Doug had been right...if he was telling the truth.

I could have bitten my tongue for even thinking such a thought. Of course, Doug was telling the truth.

At length I got into my nightgown and turned off the light. I pulled back the covers in the dark and crawled between the sheets.

CHAPTER X

Morning came, as it has a persistent way of doing, and I realized I had slept much later than I had intended to.

Sleepily, I pulled myself up and yawned repeatedly. I was out of bed, standing on the chenille rug on the floor before I saw it—a small piece of notepaper lying crumpled between the sheets.

Now what is this? I asked myself, feeling no alarm until I picked up the paper and got a good look at it. Then apprehension welled up inside me.

Really, it was absurdly melodramatic. Words had been cut from a newspaper and pasted on the small piece of notepaper. The message read: *Go away before its too late.*

My first thought was perhaps absurd. *Its* should

have had an apostrophe. Not much of a clue. Perhaps the person didn't know the rule. Perhaps the person had chosen to ignore it, or perhaps— and this was most likely—he or she simply had not quickly found the correctly punctuated contraction in the paper.

There was no doubt now that in someone's eyes I was definitely not wanted here, but no clue indicated the reason.

Perhaps it was the murderer warning me away, but the reason could also involve Grandfather's money and will. Leslie or Walter or both didn't want a family reunion to deprive them of part of their inheritance. If one of them was the murderer, he or she would have a dual reason for wanting me away.

Walter or Leslie. They always had been the prime suspects to me. I couldn't discount Rita, either. And Grandfather had sent off a letter to his exiled son just the previous morning. I had seen it, so others might have.

For a time I had harrowing visions of someone sneaking into my room as I lay fast asleep and depositing the note. But a little common sense soon dispelled those thoughts. Someone had probably pulled back the spread and placed the note on the pillow—or near the pillow—in order that I would not miss it when turning back the bed to retire. It had to have been done earlier in the evening, perhaps when I was out with Doug. But I had turned back the covers after putting out the light and had not noticed the note until morning.

If I had found it the night before, I certainly would not have slept as I had.

The future did seem ominous. I'd taken myself away from a peaceful existence and landed in the middle of a hornets' nest. And all of it had been unplanned. I had simply come to visit my grandfather. One thing had led to another, and now someone was breathing uneasily. Just as Doug had predicted.

Prudence dictated that I should consider the note the work of the murderer. That someone surely thought I was getting close. That Doug had been absolutely right when he warned me about digging into the past.

But what had I learned? A big fat zero. At most I'd gotten a somewhat different perspective on a few angles. If I had uncovered a genuine new clue, I was blind to it. I did not appear a step closer to the truth than I had been the day the terrible event took place.

What was I to do?

I cogitated over that one for a long time.

Probably I should tell Doug. But could I trust him...completely? Certainly, I would not dash down the stairs and make a general announcement and demand to know who had done the deed. Everyone would just deny it, and perhaps some would suspect that I had prepared the note myself for some weird reason.

The best course, I decided, would be to keep my eyes open and my mouth shut, which works amazingly well under a number of circumstances.

I'd scrutinize everyone very carefully and watch for any telltale signs—a certain edginess, a curious stare, a demeanor of expectation. Whoever did it would be bound to wonder about my reaction to the note.

I could have gone to the police. Only, that seemed pointless. I was young but had lived long enough in the real world to know that they weren't going to get very excited about some words pasted on paper. And there was little they could do even if they had a mind to do anything.

Then I had further thoughts about Doug. Even if I trusted him, perhaps I shouldn't tell him. He might insist on my going back home. I'd have to give the matter some thought. After all, if there was a possibility I was getting close…

The note was evidence that I was getting somewhere and I didn't want anything to happen to it. Where should I hide it? After pondering the problem a few minutes, I took down the Grandma Moses print from over the bed. Brown paper was pasted over the back side. I made a small slit at the top with a nail file and secreted the note there.

The melodramatic message had stirred me in a way nothing else had. Hastily, I bathed, dressed, and started down the stairs. Midway in my downward flight, I stopped to gain my composure.

The thing I did not need to do was to burst—filled with determination and fighting spirit—upon everyone. I needed to act natural, to act the same way I had since arriving. I counted to ten, then moved with deliberation to the kitchen.

Nina had her back to me as she scoured pans in the large sink.

"Good morning, Nina," I said.

"Oh, good morning, Miranda," she said calmly, without looking up. "There's plenty on the table."

Rita and Walter were still eating breakfast and both were sleepy-eyed. Walter wore a brown terry robe. Rita was attired in a short-sleeved silky affair, frilly and feminine. The redolence of expensive perfume mingled with the smells of coffee, bacon, and eggs. Walter slouched and yawned languidly. Rita followed suit.

"Now you're making me do it," she told him, then turned to me. "I just can't seem to get awake this morning, Miranda."

"I had some trouble myself," I told her.

"You look wide awake to me," Walter said.

"I just showered. That helps." I sat down and helped myself to some food, surreptitiously eyeing everyone else in the room. No one was sending out any signals to me. Nina worked with her usual steady efficiency. Rita and Walter seemed barely alive.

"Did you have a good time last night?" Rita asked me.

I nodded.

"What did you do?"

Walter reflected disapproval of the blunt inquiry, but I answered her question. "Went to a play, then ate at Chuck's Steakhouse."

"What kind of play did you see?"

"*Hamlet.*"

"Oh dear," she murmured. "Couldn't Doug come up with something better than that?"

"It was a little different," I told her. "It was done up in a modern setting, with modern dress, and so forth."

"Oh? I never did know what *Hamlet* was about. What is the story about, Miranda?"

I took a sip of orange juice. "Are you really interested?"

"I am."

"You're sure? It's got a humdinger of a plot, with bodies dropping everywhere. Of course, you want to remember that the plot is secondary. The majesty lies in the poetry and the—"

"Something like the Sherlock Holmes stories," Rita suggested.

"In a sense, I guess you could make the comparison. His plots—"

"His plots were for the birds," she said, interrupting once again.

Walter chimed in. "The man we are after, my dear Watson, is of Irish descent. He parts his hair in the middle, raises gerbils as a hobby, and lives in a mobile home."

"Well, he certainly couldn't raise great Danes in a mobile home," Rita told her husband. "But let's get back to *Hamlet*."

"Very well," I told her. "Hamlet is the prince of Denmark. He's been away from home and has returned after his father has been dead a month or so and his mother has married his Uncle Claudius—that is, his late father's brother."

Rita frowned, but said nothing.

I continued. "A ghost has been making a strange nightly appearance, and the ghost resembles Hamlet's late father. The ghost tells Hamlet that he—meaning Hamlet's father—had not died a natural death, but had been murdered."

It may have been my imagination, but I could almost feel a chill envelop the room upon my speaking the final word.

Rita broke the spell. "Sounds like home so far."

I went on. "The murderer was Claudius and the ghost wanted revenge. Hamlet, being the brooding and introspective sort, hems and haws and fiddle-faddles, trying to make up his mind whether the ghost is genuine. He acts strange and gets mad at his mother for marrying the possible murderer."

The others were all ears.

"Now I won't go into all the complications and deaths—but there are plenty. Anyway, one day a troupe comes to entertain and Hamlet gets an idea. He has the actors play a murder scene that's supposed to imitate the way his own father was killed. When that happens, Claudius is stricken. Hamlet knows the truth, and knows he must kill Claudius. But by accident he kills another man, Polonius, instead. So then Polonius's son wants revenge."

I paused for a breath. "It all finally comes down to a duel between Hamlet and Laertes, the son of Polonius. And Claudius has taken pains to see that Hamlet dies. He has put poison on the end of Laertes's sword and has put some more poison nearby in case Hamlet gets thirsty. Well, before it's all over, there are a lot of corpses on the floor. But

Hamlet does succeed in killing the murderer, Claudius, before he dies himself."

A hush settled over the room.

"My word!" was all Rita could manage to say.

Walter had a more pointed comment. "So it was the uncle who did it."

"Bravo!" said Leslie unexpectedly.

None of us had noticed her standing by the doorway. She came breezily into the room. "How intellectual can we get? Shakespeare for breakfast, no less. Miranda, you are too precious for words. Hamlet hemming and hawing and fiddle-faddling, indeed. I had no idea you were so keen on the bard."

"Doug took her to see *Hamlet* last night," Rita informed her sister-in-law.

"Oh? Why, what a charming idea. Most other young men would have taken her to something up-to-date."

"It was up-to-date. It was a modernized version," Rita told her.

"That is exciting then."

Rita contemplated her colorful nails. "I still think I prefer musical comedy. Don't you, Walt?"

"Musical comedy?" Walter frowned. "You know I don't like that trash. Blood-and-guts adventure is for me." He paused. "You know what they call it—there's a word. Vicarious. I take vicarious pleasure in someone else's adventure. Naturally, I don't involve myself personally in such nasty carryings-on." Fastidiously, he touched a napkin to his lips.

Grandfather came into the kitchen from the

back lawn. "What have we got here? Somebody call a family conference?"

"No, Daddy," Leslie said. "Miranda's been entertaining us with tales of Shakespeare."

"What kind of tales are you telling, girl?"

I hesitated and Walter answered for me. "Tales of murder, Dad."

"We've had enough of that," Grandfather said.

"You're right. We have," I said.

I looked all around. Everyone in the room was looking at me, including Nina, who had turned away from the sink to listen to my recital. Behind one set of eyes, I thought, lurks someone who slipped into my room and put a note under my bedspread.

My eyes moved to a little memo pad by the refrigerator. It looked like the paper used to paste the cut-outs on. Any one of them would have access to it. I lingered on the paper, but nothing suspicious showed in anyone's face. "It's time for more pleasant thoughts," I said abruptly. "The weather's cleared this morning. I think I'll enjoy the outdoors."

I struggled over my sketching for about an hour, but concentration was impossible today. My thoughts were on other matters—the note that had appeared on my bed and the feelings Doug had aroused. The attraction I felt for him—and the remaining shred of suspicion.

The afternoon I spent continuing with the reading of the county history. The material proved to be informative, amusing, and sometimes poignant, but nothing came to light about Jacob's

Corner or about anyone named Jacob or Jacobs.

With my thoughts focused on Jacob's Corner, the idea came to me that I had overlooked something pertinent. Something had recently crossed my mind, or I had heard something said that should have registered strongly. But I couldn't figure out what. Somewhere in the recesses of my mind something was waiting to be gleaned. I could not shake the feeling that had come over me.

As the day wore on, I gave more and more thought to what the night would bring and how best to cope with it. It was hard to think of any of the people at Grandfather's house as having killed Sam Roberts and harder still to imagine one of them wishing to do me real harm, their jealousies and money concerns notwithstanding. It was a case of mind over matter. My head told me that I should take care and not expose myself to danger, but my heart told me no one there could possibly hurt me.

Still, there was the note. It hadn't materialized out of the thin air. And Doug and I had agreed on the deduction: Someone at Jacob's Corner had done the deed. Of course, Doug had been at Jacob's Corner that day. Ambivalent leanings threatened to overwhelm me.

Doug called after dinner. The sound of his voice brought a little ripple of excited heartbeats, which out of their sheer unexpectedness stunned me. Oh boy, I thought. You are in danger of losing your heart. Maybe you're riding for a fall.

It really was not the sort of conversation to cause heart palpitations. Doug spoke of what he had done at work and inquired about my day. That was a big deal. I'd done a bit of sketching and had my nose stuck in a book much of the time. He said he hoped to have an evening free shortly so we could get together and "talk over strategy."

I had taken the phone call in the den. After I hung up, my mind wandered along a strange course. I started thinking about nameless voices over telephone lines, and how ordinary-sounding conversation might in reality contain coded messages of the most sinister kind. And conversely how a humorous or sarcastic choice of words might be accorded a wholly undeserved sinister quality. "Talk over strategy" was just such a phrase. A person might read an awful lot more into it than had been intended.

I took the potential seriously enough to walk very deliberately to the kitchen, just to see if anyone was around who might have lifted the receiver on the extension phone and listened in.

The kitchen was still as a tomb, eerie and still. So eerie that I felt surrounded by invisible spirits. The room seemed almost forbidding. Dishes from the evening meal had been washed and put away. Countertops were clean and uncluttered.

I had to get hold of myself.

It was nearly dark now, and the words of the note hit home with more force than ever. Certainly, I should take the words seriously enough to protect myself. Foolhardy I wasn't...I didn't think so at any rate.

The hall light was dim. I started up the stairs and paused and looked around. Why did all the shadows have a sinister aura? Why did I always feel eyes were on me?

Once I reached my room, there were preparations to make for the night. I checked things out—looked in the closet, under the bed, made certain the windows were locked, and put to good use that old standby, a chair propped under the doorknob.

Prudence, I told myself, not hysteria.

Sleep eluded me for a long time. There was too much on my mind, and concern about the unknown as well. The unknown is so much more difficult to deal with than the known. It is fraught with questions: Who? How? Where? When? Why? The why was the only one I had even an inkling about.

When it did come, sleep was not peaceful. I dreamed of the little marionettes. But the usual veil of mist had lifted, and I could see them clearly. The figures were now characters from Shakespeare's plays, each one of them a villain. There was misshapen Caliban, cruel and cunning Iago, pathetic, sleepwalking Lady Macbeth, betraying Cassius, grasping, extorting Shylock, and finally ambitious, murderous Claudius, Hamlet's uncle.

Morning was distinctly anticlimactic, a sunny day in July, just like any other. Nothing untoward had happened in the night. No noise had snatched me from my dreams to fearful wakefulness. No mysterious fingers had scrabbled at darkened windowpanes. No creaking floors had terrorized me.

I shook myself as if to throw off such unpleasant thoughts.

Life at Jacob's Corner was beginning to pull me under. I wished that I could think of whatever it was in the recesses of my mind that should tell me something important.

I needed to get away from the house for a time. I'd have to think of something to do.

I went downstairs to find Leslie at the kitchen sink. She'd braved the morning dew to pick some flowers.

"Morning," she chirruped as I strolled in. She was arranging the flowers—big daisylike blossoms on the frailest of stems. "I couldn't resist picking a bouquet this morning. They were Mama's favorite flower, you know—cosmos, the old-fashioned kind." Satisfied with the drift of pink in the narrow-necked vase, she rinsed her hands in the sink.

Lady Macbeth. The image fairly flew at me—poor Lady Macbeth trying to wash her blood-stained hands.

"Is something wrong?" my aunt asked.

I'd been staring at her. "No—no. Nothing."

"I swear, Miranda. You're getting so suspicious. The way you look at me sometimes."

"It's just the artist in me," I told her. "One observes closely."

"Well, next thing you'll have out your magnifying glass."

I poured a cup of coffee and took it out to the backyard, sat in the sun on a little camping stool, and attracted the calico cat, who rubbed against my ankles for a time, then moseyed along and stretched out in a spot of shade.

I was growing more suspicious of everyone around me. Leslie and Lady Macbeth indeed! Crisp and cheerful Leslie was a far cry from any image I'd had hitherto of Lady Macbeth. I'd put on my conjuring cap and examined each person as a likely suspect just recently and had come up virtually empty-handed. It had always come back to that locked window, which shouldn't have been locked.

I thought of Doug's theories, particularly the final one that Roberts might have secured the door himself, while the windows perhaps had been locked all along. Any of them could have committed the crime, even Nina, and, yes, it was possible Doug might have swiftly dashed into the room and done the deed.

Sane people don't go dashing into rooms, slugging other people indiscriminately over the head. I believed everyone involved to be sane. But the deed had been done, and there had to be a motive as yet undiscovered.

It seemed to me that no matter how the crime occurred whoever did it took some big risks. Yet wasn't that always the case when one committed murder? Chances were taken by the culprit and his luck had held. One might argue until doomsday that the risks were wild and foolhardy, but that would not alter the guilty one's success.

It was maddening. I had to get my mind off it all. Getting away from Jacob's Corner would do me good, and I thought of something to do. I'd go into town, to the nearby county seat, browse, perhaps shop a little, and eat lunch. And I'd go to the library and see if they had a copy of the book Doug had lent me. There ought to be an even chance they did. Surely there had not been a multitude of histories written about the county. I was pleased with myself for thinking of it.

I left the house shortly before lunchtime.

CHAPTER XI

"Escaping from the bear garden?"

I was gazing in the window of a jewelry shop, admiring some perfectly gorgeous opals, like a child eyeing a candy counter. I had recognized the voice and knew whom to expect. I turned to Doug, smiling as I did so. "How'd you guess?"

"Got lucky, I guess."

I turned back to the opals. "They say they bring bad luck, so it's just as well I don't have the money to buy them."

"That makes two of us, and we don't need any bad luck."

His lawyer duds would have been at home in the city, and I felt almost shabby by comparison in my calico skirt, sleeveless top, and sandals. But he didn't seem to notice. There was a look of distinct pleasure in his eyes.

He went on. "That all you're doing, just escaping?"

"I thought I'd do a little of this and a little of that. Perhaps do a little shopping and have some lunch."

"Would you believe I just took off for lunch? Want to come along?"

I agreed and walked along beside him toward a local diner.

It was a pleasant town with old brick buildings mingling with newer structures, and was redolent of hospitality and friendliness. The day was a nearly perfect one of blue skies and sunshine, children playing, women talking and shopping, and old men sitting on benches.

The diner was furnished with ice cream parlor tables covered with red-checked tablecloths. We ordered plebeian fare, and I told Doug I planned to go to the library in search of the missing page.

"Oh, good thinking, Miranda. You'll solve the case yet. *The Case of the Missing Page.* Sounds like Perry Mason, doesn't it?"

"You're poking fun," I protested.

"Nonsense. Lawyers don't poke fun," he said, straight-faced. "Let me know if anything fascinating turns up."

Now was the time, I thought, to tell him about the note I'd found. I drew little squares on the tablecloth with my finger. I tried, but the words wouldn't come. It was such an altogether pleasant chance meeting. I didn't want to spoil it with a sinister revelation.

And I didn't want to impose on him. He had a

job to do, and I shouldn't interfere with it by sharing my own problems with him. I'd keep it a secret a while longer. Besides, although he could not have left the note for me, he might have been involved with it in some way....

"You know, you have the deepest gray eyes I've ever seen," he said.

I snapped out of my reverie.

"You know what else? I think you're keeping something from me." There was an intensity in his own blue eyes, and they bore down on me with a quiet ferocity.

I managed an enigmatic smile. "Now you know a girl can't tell everything."

He let it pass, and the waitress soon brought us our hamburgers and iced tea. And we talked of this and that, of cabbages and kings, and why the ocean's boiling hot, and all that. He left me feeling decidedly upbeat.

After he had gone back to his law office, I walked to the public library.

The town had changed some in the years since I'd seen it, but the old stone library with its gothic arches remained the same. A silver-haired librarian smiled at me and said hello, as if I were a regular patron. My searching eyes quickly caught sight of the card index file.

A wave of satisfaction rippled through me when I came to the title I was looking for. So I had been right. They did have a copy of the book.

I found the reference section, pulled the volume from the shelf, and sat at one of the reading tables.

In looking back, I feel that I should have had a

premonition about that missing page. Some inner voice should have said to me, *What if you locate the book only to find the same sheet missing from it? Then what will you do?* But it had not. Merrily, I thumbed through the pages. Then my jaw dropped, and I pondered the very strange turn of events.

I found myself scowling furiously over the opened volume. The same page was missing. There really must have been something important on that page. The question was: Important to whom? Upon reflection, some indeterminate number of minutes later, the only harmless explanation that came to mind was that some local's great-grandfather or somesuch had committed a crime or come to shame of some sort, and the local had snipped out the evidence from all extant copies of the book in the area.

My frown turned to amusement as I envisioned someone—probably a dear little old lady much like the librarian—stealthily snipping out the offending page. *The Snipping Bandit,* I thought.

But it still seemed too much of a coincidence and both perplexed and annoyed me. All of my suspects could have done it. Including Doug.

I made a decision and rose to my feet. I carried the book over to the check-out desk and pointed out the mutilation to the elderly lady in charge. "Did you know this page was missing?" I asked her.

Her brows went up and her lips drew together. She shook her head. "Oh, dear," she uttered softly. "Oh, dear. No, I did not. It is an old book and not used very much anymore that I know of. It makes one wonder, doesn't it?" she asked, her eyes twinkling. "One really wants to know what was on the missing page much more than one is interested in all the rest that's here. It's very mysterious."

I smiled. "Yes, it is rather. I would like to know what was on the missing page."

"I shall take the matter up with Mrs. Ferguson, our head librarian," she averred.

That was all very well, I thought, but it wasn't getting me the page to read.

The woman expressed heartfelt thanks that I felt were undeserved. I turned to leave and took a few steps.

"Oh, miss," she called.

I swung around. "Yes."

"It's just a thought I had. I know someone who might have a copy of the book, if you'd be interested."

"Oh? Actually, I would be."

She held a frail didactic finger aloft. "Hazel Mesmering."

"Hazel Mesmering?"

"Yes. Her father had so many books, and I know some were histories of Ohio and the area hereabouts. She has a big old three-section bookcase, monstrous really, full of his books. Possibly, she'd have a copy of this one. Would you like me to check with her?"

"Do you think she'd mind?"

"Not at all. Hazel is amenable—about most things. Annoy her Siamese cat Wung Ho or Ho Chung or whatever and she's not in the least amenable!" With that, the librarian checked her telephone book and began to dial.

The lady under discussion was soon on the other end of the line. After a brief flurry of preliminaries, the problem at hand was presented and an accord reached.

The silver-haired woman put down the phone. She looked up with a beaming smile. "She thinks she just may have the book. At the moment she must leave her house to attend a club meeting, but as soon as she returns home, she'll check. If you'll be so good as to call her about seven tonight, she'll let you know." She proceeded to write down the telephone number.

"I can't thank you enough," I told her.

"That's quite all right," she said modestly. "Now, if the page is missing from Hazel's book, we will have a mystery on our hands, won't we?"

"No doubt about it."

It was already a mystery to me, but I knew I shouldn't go off half-cocked, casting beyond the moon. By dint of perseverance, I'd get my information soon enough. Meantime, I'd remain calm and just wait and see what happened.

I did some shopping, buying a hand-tooled leather belt, browsed, then returned to Jacob's Corner around four o'clock.

Grandfather and Leslie were standing under the big old sycamore in the front when I drove up. They seemed to be discussing the state of the crab apple trees.

Leslie spoke to me. "We were beginning to

wonder about you. Daddy was afraid you'd been kidnapped."

"Don't be worrywarts. Whoever would want to kidnap me?"

Grandfather smiled. "Why, young Doug might."

"I hardly think that would be necessary," Leslie said.

I went into the house without comment.

Then I ran smack into Rita in the entry hall. As was her custom, she wanted to know what I had done, whom I had seen, and what I had bought.

I showed her the belt and she admired it, running her long, brightly colored nails over its intricate surface.

"It didn't take you that long just to buy a belt," she observed.

"No, I made the rounds, had lunch, browsed through several shops, looked around at the library."

"You're always up to cultural things, aren't you?"

"Maybe I'm just an egghead."

"That's one thing nobody will ever accuse me of."

I went on past Rita and down the hall to the kitchen to see if there was something cold to drink.

Nina was making noodles. She looked up as I opened the refrigerator. "What a nosy Parker that woman is," she said with disapproval.

Nina had not forgiven Rita for the breakfast bombshell.

"People like that never change," I said. "Not much use in getting discombobulated whenever they pry."

"You're just so right about that," Nina said thoughtfully. "Most people don't change. They go through life doing the same thing over and over."

Sad but true. In my mind's eye, I could see Rita in her golden years, her auburn locks turned to silver—or perhaps they would still be auburn—still blurting out the same insensitive questions. And I could see Walter in his dotage, still looking for the gold at the end of the rainbow.

But more pressing than my thoughts of Rita and Walter were my thoughts of the call to Mrs. Mesmering.

When the phone rang, I was standing nearby and answered it. I really hadn't expected it to be Doug.

"What are you doing?" he asked.

"Nothing much," I told him. "Thinking about Rita and Walter in their dotage."

Nina sniggered in a subdued fashion, and I glanced surreptitiously around to make sure neither one was within earshot.

"That sounds like a depressing thought. I was wondering if you'd like to have supper with me. I know this is getting to be a habit. You see, I'm doing a survey on the eating habits of Chicagoans when they come out to the hinterlands."

"Oh, you are, are you?" I said with a laugh.

"Yes, and I know this place down the road where you hardly ever get ptomaine poisoning. Do you think you'd like to take your chances?"

"If you're game, I guess I am."

I replaced the receiver and went out of the kitchen, only to meet Leslie coming down the hall.

"Aren't you all bright-eyed and bushy-tailed this evening," she said gaily.

Thereupon Rita appeared and said, "Why not? The girl's entitled to a little romance."

"Really now. I haven't been here a week. I'm not that impetuous."

"I don't know," Leslie murmured, the calculating gleam in her green eyes.

"Going out again tonight?" Rita asked.

"As a matter of fact, I am."

"Hmmm. Must be nice," Rita said.

I thought it was rather nice myself, although it was none of their business, and I didn't let on. Instead, I went upstairs to make myself presentable before Doug arrived.

Anyway, light conversation wasn't exactly my cup of tea at the moment. Too many mysteries were connected with Jacob's Corner and its residents to suit me. A man had been murdered here. Pages had strangely disappeared from perfectly innocuous books which had just recently passed through my hands. Someone definitely wanted me away.

There was still that nagging something buried in my mind that I couldn't recall yet felt had a bearing on the mysteries. It bugged me that I couldn't put a finger on it.

CHAPTER XII

The little spot Doug took me to wouldn't have won a prize from the country's leading gourmet, but it was respectable looking and the food seemed well prepared. Doug was famished and had ordered a big steak and potatoes.

"Don't you get enough to eat?" I asked him. "I'll inveigle an invitation for you to Grandfather's, and you can load up on some of Nina's cooking."

"Nina's cooking is something I'm able to tolerate right well. But I'm really a fair cook myself. Let's just say I have other enticements for eating out lately."

"An enticement? Am I an enticement? That makes me feel like a girl in a billboard saying, 'Use this brand—it's better.'"

Doug seemed amused by the thought I had

expressed. He flashed his half grin and chuckled to himself. "You're in good spirits tonight," he said. "Things must be going better at the bear garden."

"I've been staying away more."

"Did you enjoy yourself in town this afternoon?" he asked.

"Very much."

His eyes met mine, and there was something in his look that made me vaguely uncomfortable. This thing might be rushing along too swiftly. If I didn't take care I'd be falling head over heels. And—taking everything into consideration—I couldn't afford to do that. For Doug was still one of my suspects.

I changed the subject. "The afternoon was more than enjoyable, Doug. There was a surprise element."

"Oh?" He spooned sour cream over his baked potato.

I nodded. "You remember, I told you I intended to go to the library to see if they had a copy of that book you loaned me, the one with the missing page?"

"Uh-huh. So they had it, huh?" His voice seemed a trifle grim.

I nodded again. "Yes, they had it." With my fingertips I lightly tapped out a tune on the tabletop. "But what do you think about this?" I leaned forward. "The same page had been cut out of that book, too."

"Oh now, you're putting me on." Was he really surprised? Or was he faking?

"Really. It was missing."

Doug was the lawyer instantly, scrutinizing me with his intense eyes that scrutinized so well. "You've got a real flair for mysteries, haven't you, girl?"

I smiled at his deliberate use of my grandfather's pet appellation for me. "It's strange, isn't it, Doug?" I took a dainty bite of tomato from my tossed salad.

"It is, for a fact."

"I've thought of possible explanations," I said.

"I knew you would."

"How does this theory strike you? You do want to hear about my theory, don't you? Try this on for size. Somewhere along the vast expanse that is called the Ohio River there lurks a quote Snipping Bandit unquote."

His brows knitted. He cut off a piece of steak. But he continued to listen attentively.

I went on. "I thought perhaps that page contained a reference to a misdeed of someone's ancestor. Perhaps it was a crime, or perhaps just some peccadillo. It may have had something to do with the abolition cause. Maybe some man got put in jail for violating the Fugitive Slave Law, or—or maybe a woman's virtue was maligned in order to get even with her for her activities. I could think of lots more—"

"So someone has been sneaking around, creeping into bookcases, bowdlerizing in their own fashion?" He was grinning fully now. "What a wild imagination you have, Miranda. And you know what? It's a crazy enough theory to be perfectly true."

"Yes, I suppose. But I really don't think that's the case," I admitted. "Whatever it is, I think it hits a lot closer to home." I gritted my teeth. "I think someone didn't want *me* to see what was on that missing page. There's surely some kind of evidence there."

"I'd have to agree, in part at least." He was speaking very slowly, I thought. "It's evidence of something, like the trout in the milk. Did you mention the missing page to anyone at the house?"

"No."

"Tell anyone you were going to the library?"

I thought back. "No, I'm sure I didn't." I glanced at the clock on the wall. "I just may have some solutions pretty soon now," I said.

He gave me a questioning look.

"I may have found another copy of the book. There was this sweet old biddy at the library who—oh, never mind all that. To make a long story short, the librarian contacted a woman named Hazel Mesmering, who thinks she may have a copy. I'm going to call her pretty soon."

"Hazel, huh?"

"Uh-huh. Do you know her?"

He shrugged. "Slightly. She once wanted to sue her neighbors. Claimed their target practice was making her cat neurotic. I had to sweet talk her out of that."

"Sounds like a character. Is that your specialty with the law firm—sweet talk?"

He smiled. "I serve where I'm called. Hazel's a character, also a sweet old biddy." He was eyeing his empty coffee cup and our waitress, who was chatting with another waitress.

"I think I'll call Hazel now, before I have my dessert. Don't mind, do you? If you're able to flag down our girl, have her give me some coffee, too. Gee, I hope the phone works."

"Miracles do happen," he said and looked hopefully toward the waitress.

I walked to the pay phone in the corner.

Very soon after I dialed, a gracious voice said hello. When I had identified myself, the voice said, "My dear, I am so pleased that I can be of help to you. As I thought, I do have a copy of the book in question—an intact copy."

I could sense excitement in the voice.

"Your page numbered 167 and 168 is here."

I made delighted exclamations.

"It's most interesting, by the way," the gracious woman told me. "I'm sorry I've never delved into the book before."

"You've read the page then?"

"Front and back. It's about people who worked for the Underground Railroad—conductors, the author calls them. There are several names mentioned, but I rather think the one that will interest you is that of a rather mysterious man, a man from this locality. His name was Jacob Schumacher."

Suddenly my heart was hammering. All I could hear was the name Jacob repeating itself over and over like the beat of a jungle tom-tom.

"Miss? Are you still there? The author says Mr.

Schumacher lived near the river, and legend has it he kept a lantern burning at night in an upper window as a sort of beacon to runaway slaves. Most interesting, I must say, and I thought you would find it interesting also."

I found it interesting...*exciting...tantalizing*....

Then I found my tongue to thank the gracious voice at the other end and to promise I'd come by the following day to read the text in full, if that was all right, which it was. Slowly, I replaced the receiver.

"Ay, now the plot thickens very much upon us," was the quote running through my brain. I couldn't stop it. It flashed off and on like a neon sign. With a slight giddiness, I walked back to our table.

"You found out something," was all Doug said, but a noticeable liquidity of his blue eyes indicated a whetting of his interest.

I spoke slowly. "She has the book, Doug. It's intact. The missing page tells about a man named Jacob."

He laid his fork down abruptly. "Oh, now, is that a fact?"

I went on to give him the sketchy information the woman had provided me with. "Doug—it fits, it fits, it fits," I ended.

He rubbed his chin and remained more composed than I. "So our Jacob did more than sell apples or squashes. Yes, it does fit. It would seem that your Jacob's Corner has a history worth looking into. But aside from that, I don't see that there was anything earthshaking revealed."

"But why would anyone tear out the page?"

"It beats me. I gave up trying to figure out people long ago. Eat your pie, Miranda. I think it's homemade. And please notice that I've success-fully procured a refill on your coffee."

"Thank you." I did take a small bite, but little gears were turning in my brain. "I'll go over to her house and read the page front and back myself. Maybe there's something else there. That'll be a start. I wonder if it's too late to go by and read it tonight?"

"I'll take you if you feel you have to see it, Miranda. The lady lives about ten miles from here."

I debated. "Perhaps I shouldn't. I did tell her tomorrow. Older people go to bed early some-times, don't they? With the cows, or is it the chickens?"

"Whew! All these cosmic questions you come up with," Doug said.

"I guess I'd better wait. I do hope there's something more on the page, though. There must be a clue to something there. I'm kind of pinning my hopes on it."

"So pin your hopes, but for now eat your pie."

I acquiesced and nibbled at the pie.

"Good girl. How did you ever get along without me?"

Our eyes met, but I chose to remain silent.

"Apparently, you've made out very well without me. A sharp gal with a bright future, overly curious, tends to dramatize—" He stopped abruptly. "I'm sorry. I shouldn't have said that. You've had drama in your life you never asked for."

"I'm not the only one. That's life, I guess."

"Philosophizes, too," he continued.

I broke into a smile. "Are you quite finished?"

"Not really. Has the deepest gray eyes I ever saw. Surprised I've turned out to be the romantic?"

"Well, I must admit there was a time when I thought of you as anything but."

"And you were right. There were lots of times when I needed a good kick in the pants."

"Don't we all?"

We devoted some words then to nostalgic recollections of old times and had a laugh or two. Then we left the restaurant and drove around the area for a while. Doug pointed out some of the many changes that had taken place in the county since I had last been there.

Throughout the evening I kept telling myself that I really ought to tell Doug about the note that had been left on my bed, that I really ought to trust him completely. But each time I started to say something, the words simply would not come, and the evening passed into my memory with the deed still undone.

We arrived back at Grandfather's early, before eleven. Tonight there was no romantic tattoo of rain upon the automobile. But, stepping out of the car, I thought the mulled night air had a charm of its own. Doug walked me to the door.

"Would you like to come in?" I asked him.

"No. I'm already close to becoming your grandfather's star boarder as it is."

"I don't think Grandfather objects."

"No. Perhaps not. But I've got some reading to do. I usually do have. I'd…better go."

"Whatever you think, but—uh—anytime you have a few free moments, give a little thought to my curious discovery and what it can mean and how it can fit in," I said.

He was close to me, and I could see a starry spot of moonlight in his eyes.

"You never give up, do you?" he murmured. And I thought of his warnings to leave the past alone. Then he took me by the shoulders and I forgot everything but his nearness. Tonight the kiss seemed right, and I had no objections to it, none whatsoever.

We said good night and I slipped inside.

A light burned dimly in the hall, but no one stirred. It appeared that all had retired, so I flicked off the switch, darkening the downstairs. Upstairs, a low-watt lamp still burned and some of its illumination poured downward, but its effect was shadowy, almost ominous, and it made me uneasy. It made me feel I was being watched.

Hastily, I started up the steps. Midway up, I thought I heard a creak that had not come from my own feet. I paused and looked behind me and all around. Again, I had the feeling someone was watching me. Overactive imagination, I told myself but scooted quickly up to my room. I was coming down with a good case of the creeps. It was going to be that kind of night.

I checked out my room very carefully and lodged a chair beneath the doorknob.

Once safety precautions had been taken, I

turned my thoughts to Doug and to my growing fondness for him. I wondered. Was I making a fool of myself? I didn't know very much about him really. He didn't seem like a ladies' man looking for a new conquest, but people aren't always what they seem. And there was still the unfinished business here....

Oh, I was being foolish even to think such a thing. Doug was exactly what he seemed to be, and I did like him very much. Yet he did have a very good chance to tear out that offending page from both books....

No, I must stop being so suspicious! For a time I pushed thoughts of Doug into a backwater of my mind. There was no shortage of subjects to occupy my thoughts at the moment.

I walked to the window that overlooked the river. The light was on in my room and I could see but little of the night. Pressing my face up close to the glass, however, I could see bright stars overhead, a patch of sheen below, and between the two a tangled darkness.

Once again, the thrill of discovery left me fluttery on the inside. Mrs. Mesmering had said...Surely it fit. Surely. How many Jacobs might there have been who lived in a house overlooking the river?

Could it be that Jacob Schumacher burned his lantern from this very window as a signal light to any fleeing soul able to make it across the river? I rested my hands upon the sill. I almost felt as if I could reach all the way to the past and experience the pain, anxiety, exuberance, all the vagaries of emotion that must have permeated Jacob's Corner at one time.

And had Jacob Schumacher once stood on this very spot, even as I, and peered into the gloom, wondering when next and under what circumstances his clandestine services might be required? I could almost feel the warmth of his hand resting where mine lay now. From my vantage point the river seemed but a whimsical shimmer laid under a glittery canopy, a dark painting rendered in silver and sequined. But at closer range it would appear a treacherous thing to ford, very treacherous indeed. I wondered how many runaways had attempted to swim its breadth, and how many had succeeded. Frozen over in the winter, it might be easier to cross. But nevertheless it would be a frigid and dangerous journey.

My thoughts flew to *Uncle Tom's Cabin*. It was across the ice-clogged Ohio River that Eliza escaped, carrying her young son, while Uncle Tom went on to a cruel fate at a different plantation from the one she fled. The scene, when portrayed on the stage, had been one of great melodrama. But it had happened, no doubt, in much the same way to real people, and the fear gripping them had been as real as the rain that falls and the wind that blows.

Perhaps I did have a flair for the dramatic. There had been drama in my life, a continuing drama. Things had happened to me that do not happen to everyone.

Still, I found the association of Jacob's Corner with the activities of the Underground Railroad mind-boggling. Tingles of excitement coursed through me. And more.

In some way the past of Jacob's Corner had to be linked with its present. Its past posed a threat to someone. There had to be a reason why those pages had been snipped away. A station on the Underground Railroad and a present-day murder. A thread linked the two. I felt certain of it.

It was all very well for Doug to question the connection. Doug didn't know the whole truth. Or was he—was he the only one who did? I'd never brought myself to tell him about the little note of warning. If I couldn't trust him completely, could I trust anyone?

Suddenly I felt terribly isolated. I shared a house with five others, yet I felt alone.

The vision of little marionettes came to me once again. This time it had a few new twists. One of those little figures had planted a note telling me to go away. The same figure that had carefully snipped away the identical page from two copies of the same book?

How could I determine at what point the individual would shrink from further action? Intuitively, I failed to sense, at the bone-marrow level, a genuine personal danger. Perhaps I just could not accept the thought that someone connected with Jacob's Corner could actually do me harm. Had I been beguiled? How did I know there was not a person nearby who would stop at nothing to keep me from learning the truth?

I didn't.

The attempt to drive me away did seem

halfhearted at best. Why no concerted effort to terrorize me into leaving? Why no follow-up to the solitary message? Could it be that the guilty one had mixed feelings about me? Or could it be that my nameless nemesis had little patience? Could it be that I could expect one warning, and nothing more? It was a frightening thought.

Sam Roberts had turned his back on someone. Obviously, he had not done so with the expectation of being struck down with a poker. I should not allow myself to be lulled into such a sense of false security.

And so it came down to another night of caution, of a door secured by an old chair, of a second check of windows and of possible hiding places.

There was still that elusive something that had passed the threshold of my brain. But I had let it get away from me and it seemed as slippery as any fish in the sea.

At last I settled down to an uneasy sleep. The morning could come none too quickly to suit me.

CHAPTER XIII

The morning began with the commonplace.

Grandfather and Leslie were just finishing their breakfast when I came down to the kitchen. Nina hastened to prepare some hot food for me. Within minutes she had folded over a luscious-looking omelet and served it with hot biscuits and link sausages.

"You must think I'm undernourished," I told her.

Nina smiled indulgently, as if she possessed superior knowledge of such matters as proper eating habits, and spoke not a single word.

"Eat up," Grandfather commanded me. "It'll give you the strength you need for carousing with Doug."

"Now, Daddy, I don't think carousing is a very good word to use," Leslie said.

"Well, maybe not, but I used to carouse myself, a little, before I met your mother." Grandfather lifted his favorite cup to his lips and seemed very pleased with himself for his little confession.

I found myself smiling indulgently at my grandfather. It's so difficult to imagine an older person as once having been young and capable of carousing, especially when the person happens to be your father's father.

"I can see you don't believe me, girl."

"I believe you, Grandfather," I said.

"It's an idea that takes some getting used to, that I was once young, eh? Lots of new ideas nowadays that take some getting used to for me. I was a fairly handsome feller, you know."

"You were every bit as handsome as Doug Lassiter," Leslie told him. "I've seen all the old pictures."

"That was a long, long time ago," Grandfather told her. He seemed to slip away from us and go back in his thoughts to meander along the path to times past.

As I set to work on the omelet, Rita came into the kitchen. "Gosh," she said, looking at the clock, "only eight. I just can't understand why I woke up oh so early. It isn't like me at all."

Grandfather slowly shook his head. "Rita," he said, "you sure wouldn't make any farmer's wife."

"I should say not," she said, almost indignantly. "Nobody'll ever catch me getting up at the crack of dawn and slopping the pigs. What a dreadful thought."

"I don't think you'll ever need to worry about that," Grandfather said. "You and Walter are two of a kind—just like two little green peas in a pod."

"Yes, we are. We are compatible, aren't we? Walter would never turn to anything like farm work."

There was an extra word in her final sentence, but I was agreeable and didn't point out the fact to Rita.

And so the talk went at breakfast, ordinary chitchat.

I chatted along with the others, but primarily my thoughts were on an entirely differcnt level, a level in which mystery and possible treachery were involved.

Doug called me shortly after breakfast, and I found my feelings to be jumbled indeed. A thrill that was fast becoming familiar swept through me at the sound of his voice, and my fondest recollection at that moment was that of the kiss of the night before.

"How're ya doin'?" was the less-than-romantic way he greeted me over the phone.

"How're ya doin' yourself?" I responded. "Me, I made it through the night."

"You sound as if that was an unexpected development."

"Well, around here one never knows."

"I take it everything is all right, then—as right as can be reasonably expected."

"Yes, as far as I can tell. Everything seems normal—for Jacob's Corner."

"Just thought I'd check things out."

I thought it was sweet of him to call to check on things. That was my first thought. Then all the recent fears and uncertainties came back.

For the next hour I did very little. I merely whiled away the time waiting for a decent hour to call upon Mrs. Mesmering in order to get a gander at the missing page.

The doorbell sounded. I answered it to find—lo and behold—that Doug stood before me. "My, but don't you pop up unexpectedly," I greeted him. It was a pleasant surprise.

A book tucked under his arm instantly caught my eye.

"Let's go somewhere to talk," he said.

"Where would you suggest? Our trysting place is being redecorated just now."

"In rare form, aren't you? Let's just sit in the car. That'll throw everyone off the track. If we get in the back seat, they'll just question your virtue."

We climbed into the front seat, however, and Doug handed the book to me. "I made a call to Mrs. Mesmering this morning," he told me. "She loaned me the book to show to you. I'd spent the night racking my brain trying to figure out how it all fits in."

"Welcome to the club," I said, taking the book.

It was exciting having the much-sought-after page in my hands at last. I devoured the words as Doug sat silently beside me.

In a sense the reading proved anticlimactic.

In the area of human cooperation, the Underground Railroad had been one of the most astounding projects ever undertaken. Totally lacking in formal organization, it nevertheless managed to function efficiently. But much of its workings would always be cloaked in secrecy. Records and personal accounts of the endeavor were few and far between.

Of the various people mentioned, Jacob Schumacher received but scant attention. There was very little known about him. The author said he was a prosperous farmer who had long been considered a local kingpin of the Railroad. But Jacob never talked, nor had he kept a journal.

Around 1840 he had built a home overlooking the river. The author added that certain slaves across the river in Kentucky had spoken in hushed tones of "Jacob's ladder." To know what this ladder consisted of one had to use one's imagination. It was a part of a world of secret river crossings, mysterious signals, hidden footpaths, and clever hiding places.

Having completed the passage, I winced. "I'd hoped there'd be more."

"So had I," Doug admitted.

"There has to be a connection, though. Don't you agree?"

Doug drummed his fingers thoughtfully on the steering wheel. "Like I've said, the same page torn from the same two books is evidence of something, like a trout in the milk. But evidence of what?"

"How many people would have had access to the book at your place or Reverend Garrity's?" I asked him.

He shrugged. "No telling. Not so many at my place, but half the county trooped through his house when Thomas was alive. I've thought about that angle myself, but I kind of feel like I brought the book over here intact."

I nodded. "I think so, too. That page has to implicate someone in some way, someone here at Jacob's Corner. And—well, I know for a fact somebody wants me away from here."

The corners of his eyes slanted down. "Now just how do you know that?"

I gulped. "I should have told you earlier. I meant to, but I couldn't. I mean, I was afraid you'd just want me to leave, or—or something. Well, anyway, someone left a little note in my room the other night. It was Monday—the evening we went to the play. The message was on notepaper from the kitchen and very melodramatically told me to go away before it's too late."

He clapped the heel of his hand to his forehead. "You didn't say a word to me!"

I was being meek. "I didn't know what it meant. I thought maybe Walter or Rita or Leslie—"

"They what?"

"Well…I don't know exactly what I thought. I just don't think they were too keen on my coming here. If Dad reconciles with Grandfather, I suppose Grandfather will change his will again— he said once he was disinheriting Dad—and the estate will go three ways instead of two. I don't think they want to see that happen. Oh, in time they'll accept it, I suppose."

"Mercenary bunch, your relatives."

"It's just human nature, I guess. If I had felt real danger, I'd have told you about the note, or I'd have left immediately. Something tells me I'm not in real danger."

"I wonder if anything told Roberts that?"

There was no gainsaying it. That sentiment echoed some thoughts I'd already had. But I said, "Roberts was a con man, a shifty one who'd probably have cheated his mother if he had the chance. Whoever did it must have had a good reason to do him in."

"Do you really think someone who has killed once would hesitate to do it again?" Doug asked.

"The popular theory would be that a person becomes inured to murder, so that each additional killing becomes easier. But I think a person might feel so much remorse over doing such a thing that they would never be able to do it again, a person with a conscience, that is."

"The shrinks can grapple with that one. I'll just pass, if you don't mind. In the meantime, Miranda, someone believes you're getting close to something. *Go away before it's too late.*" He shook his head.

I opened my mouth.

"Even if you aren't close, Miranda, you've succeeded in seeming to push someone into a corner, and you've got to be prepared for them to come out swinging. I hate to say I told you so, but I did."

"What can I do? There's nothing the police can do. They'd probably think I created the message myself in an attempt to show that my dad really was innocent. I want to prove Dad innocent. I don't want to go away."

"Your father has been found innocent by a jury of his peers, Miranda," he reminded me. "I know that's not enough for you. You want the guilty party found out." He rubbed his chin. "I don't really want you to go away," he continued softly. "On the other hand, I can't have you going about your business willy-nilly and further endangering your own life. By the way, did you get any ideas from the handwriting on the note?"

"No. It wasn't written by hand. They cut out newspaper words and pasted them on the paper. Doug, what do you think Jacob's ladder is?"

He looked at me with some disapproval for changing the subject. He pondered. "I don't know. Probably it's a metaphor. Jacob's ladder led to heaven, didn't it?"

"Yes. I see what you mean. This Jacob's ladder led to freedom. I could believe such an allusion."

He nodded. "So there's not a heck of a lot to go on.

"Somebody's giving me a lot more credit for cleverness than I deserve," I said.

"But what's important is that somebody thinks you have discovered something, or discerned something, or are about to. Miranda, I want you to promise me you'll take extra precautions today."

"Promise not to turn my back on any Calvins?"

"It might not be a bad idea."

"I'll be careful, believe me, Doug. But nothing else has happened. There haven't been any additional threats. I don't understand it. What are we going to do?"

"That I don't know. I wish I did. I'll be over tonight. Right now, I've got to get to the office. I have to work on a brief. Tonight we'll talk. I may bring everything out in the open and see what kind of a reaction we get."

"You'll get a reaction, I'm sure, if you do that. Calvins are known for their reactions."

Doug left shortly after that and I went in to face some questioning glances. Everybody seemed keenly interested in Doug's early-morning call and in my activities. I didn't give anyone, not even Rita, a chance to interrogate me. Quickly, I went up the stairs to my room.

Once again, the window lured me. I stood looking out over the river bathed in bright sunshine, but I still felt a surge of excitement over the thought that perhaps from that very window the dedicated abolitionist Jacob Schumacher burned his signal lamp.

Jacob Schumacher and his ladder to freedom.

I began to speculate about the man and his whimsical ladder. What if Doug had been wrong? What if the ladder had been a literal one instead of a figurative one? Where would such a device have been located?

The presence of a ladder meant one thing: going up. Somewhere someone had used a ladder to go up. Then a second thought occurred to me: or it meant going down. A ladder would be used for going up or going down. Up or down. I thought of all the places where one might go up or down.

Once I had put my mind to such ponderings, a vast number of possibilities presented themselves.

A ladder could lead to so many places. It could have led to a hiding place in a large tree, in this case perhaps referring to a rope ladder to pull up after oneself. I scanned the treetops and wondered if such a hiding place might be possible. I failed to see anything that seemed suitable. The huge old sycamore in the front was the largest tree I knew of. It was a landmark, but I had no way of knowing whether it had been standing all those many years before. Perhaps another big old tree had been used and was no longer standing today.

A barn or other outbuilding was another possibility to consider, but it wasn't one that gave me any encouragement. Whatever Jacob Schumacher had built in the way of outbuildings, he had not built a two-car garage. A man who could afford to build such a house had probably owned horses and a carriage or at least some sort of utilitarian vehicle. He would have needed a stable and/or a barn. I scowled. In the intervening years all of that had been swept away. It was gone and in its stead stood a modern garage.

The house itself was more promising. A large dwelling, it must have offered myriad hiding places for the ingenious Jacob Schumacher.

I turned around then and mused with my back to the window panes.

Everyone said the original structure was basically intact. The two downstairs rooms at the back—the kitchen and a utility room—had been added later. They were tacked on almost like an afterthought, but nothing I knew of had been torn away. I set my mind to thinking of all the places where a person might hide within the walls of Jacob's Corner.

As a ladder indicates up or down, the attic and basement seemed logical places to begin the search. By now I was possessed by enough curiosity to actually embark upon a search of the premises.

I stepped into the hallway and looked furtively around. Then I moved to the opposite side where a door was set at the far end, cutting into the bedroom Nina now occupied. Here a narrow passage led up to the attic.

It did seem a bit spooky, but I shut the outer door and went on up, feeling for the light switch beside the door at the top of the stairs. I flicked it on. Inside that door, a bare bulb illuminated the unfinished, peaked interior of the attic. For a time I just stood and looked around.

The two big chimneys dominated the attic space. The mortared heaps of bricks appeared slanted, as if the mason had worked with an erring eye. But Grandfather had told me once the chimneys were built that way for a purpose. They had certainly stood the test of time, I thought.

Overhead, the large old hand-hewn rafters and tie beams were visible, just as they had been the day the house was completed. And beneath my feet were the same old rough joists.

It was like stepping into the past up here. The only additions to the original structure, that I could see, were the rolls of insulation between the joists, and the electrical wiring. No one had ever seen fit to modernize beyond those two necessities.

Ventilation openings admitted scant light, and the air, though circulating somewhat, seemed warm.

Gingerly, I moved over the joists toward the middle, where I could stand up straight without bumping my head. I walked around the chimneys and touched the old bricks, which felt cool to my hands.

The single bare bulb near the door didn't illuminate very well, and I wasn't even certain what I was looking for. Something out of place, I supposed. Something that wasn't as it should be.

It appeared that the only way up to the attic was via the narrow passage that was in plain sight. A trap door in the floor was an intriguing idea. But it would have to lead somewhere. I'd noticed the ceilings in all the bedrooms at one time or other. There weren't any places where such a thing might be let down. I wasn't up to disarranging all that insulation in search of a trap door that had no place to go to.

I went out and shut off the attic light, then went cautiously back down the stairs and ultimately on to the ground floor.

A door in the kitchen led to the basement. Nina was busy polishing some copper utensils and saw me go down, but she showed no reaction. After all, what was unusual about a person going down to the basement? If she had suspected I was looking for a mysterious ladder connected with the Underground Railroad, she probably would have raised an eyebrow, at the least.

I was glad none of the others saw me. They would likely be right on my heels, prying with not-so-subtle questions.

Grandfather had not been the sort to impress people with wall-to-wall carpeting on the basement floor and expensive paneling on the walls. This basement looked like a basement. The walls were concrete block and the floor was stone. It was not a large area, encompassing only what seemed to be the space under the dining room and Grandfather's bed-sitting room.

In Schumacher's day it probably had been even more primitive, perhaps a dirt-floor root cellar. The masonry of the chimneys extended all the way down here, for support, and the one under the dining room had held a fireplace itself. I supposed a fire in the cellar had served a useful purpose, such as an aid to lard rendering or lye making. Now it was completely closed off and I believed it had been before Grandfather bought the house.

I looked all around, at the furnace, the sump pump, various stored items. A hatchway led to the outside. It had been improved within recent years, but I believed it had been an original feature. Probably it had been the only original means of entry and exit, because the kitchen hadn't been built yet.

Left unlocked, the hatchway would have provided entry for a runaway slave, I mused. From that point my vivid imagination needed no prodding. I could see a damp and dark cellar, meanly furnished with the barest essentials—a pallet on the floor, a lantern, a larder of sorts supplied with food. Perhaps the cellar fireplace had served more to warm fugitive bodies than to aid in household chores.

So, then, was that all Jacob's ladder consisted of—steps leading into a cellar?

Puzzling, I frowned. It wasn't the sort of thing I'd had in mind. Something ingenious—and, yes, spectacular—would have been more to my liking.

It did seem to me that there should have been more. A secret chamber perhaps, or another means of entrance or exit. Surely a dedicated conductor for the Underground would have taken further measures to insure the safety of his temporary charges.

Looking all around, it was hard to imagine any secret hiding place down there. I reminded myself, however, that it had been many, many years since Jacob Schumacher had walked the floors of Jacob's Corner, and a lot of changes could have taken place since that time.

Back up the steps I trudged. I went out of the kitchen and stood gazing up and down the hall. The staircase was an open one. A closed one might have offered a potential for a hiding place. Opposite the kitchen side where I stood, a narrow passage led first to a utility room, then to a bath. As these rooms had been added at a much later time, I wondered if a hiding place had existed at the rear of the house, to be subsequently destroyed by the renovation.

How perplexing it was. It was hard to believe there was a connection between the activities so long ago of Jacob Schumacher and the present unsolved murder. But it seemed that someone at least thought there was, thus making it incumbent upon me to make whatever discovery was waiting to be unearthed.

I went out the back door and walked slowly around the house studying the old brick walls and continuing to cudgel my brain for an idea, any sort of idea. Presently, I was back where I started, just outside the back door, and devoid of fresh inspiration.

I went back up to my room feeling as if I had profited not a whit by all my morning activities.

Still possessed by curiosity, however, I plopped down in the rocker by my bed, leaned back, and lost myself in thought. Somewhere in the house there had to be a clue, surely.

I sat staring at the paneled chimney wall, and it was the merest happenstance that I began to wonder…and wonder.

There was something I had to satisfy myself about. I got my flashlight out of a drawer and went down to the den.

CHAPTER XIV

There was so much stored in the bottom of the big cherry corner cupboard!

I opened up both doors at the bottom and proceeded to set out items on the floor. There was crockery, some old cobalt blue bottles, several fairly old books, a paperweight, old paper fans with Chinese scenes, extension cords, trivets, a mason jar filled with nuts and bolts, and so on. The number of articles seemed endless.

The doorbell chimed. I paid no heed to it at all until I recognized Doug's voice out in the hall. Surprised, I started to get up, but Leslie, who had let him in, told him I was in the den and opened the door. I had not realized anyone in the house knew where I was, although I should have known better than that.

Leslie's brows furrowed as she glanced at the

sight of me on the floor in the midst of the melange of contents just removed from the cupboard.

"Our lawyer friend is burning up the road this morning," she told me. To Doug she said, "You'll have to ask her what she's doing. She's very mysterious today."

The calico cat had taken advantage of the opened door to sneak in. She padded between the feet of Leslie and Doug, selected a straight-back chair, tucked her paws beneath her body, and proceeded to keep an eye on happenings.

"You are burning up the road, in addition to the telephone lines," I told him.

Doug murmured something about two great minds with one thought, and he began to assist me. He cleared a space by moving items farther away. Then he reached into the back of the cupboard for what items yet remained inside.

"I thought you had a brief to work on," I told him.

"I sneaked out while the big cheese was in court—more important things to do. I have to help my girl solve a mystery. You have brought out the Perry Mason in me, Miranda."

And now I'm your girl, I thought and wished I had the time to ponder his words.

Out in the hall Grandfather was calling to Leslie and wanting to know who had come into the house. She stepped out of the room and quickly reappeared with Grandfather at her side. They stood in the doorway.

Doug looked up. "You don't mind my dismantling your cupboard, do you, Cyrus?"

Grandfather gave him a long, squinty look and merely said, "Well, I think I'd better keep an eye on you, son. I always do that when somebody starts to dismantle my house." He pulled up a chair with a good deal of nonchalance and sat down to observe the proceedings himself.

Rita drifted in, followed by Walter, then by Nina.

"What's this?" Walter asked, a look of sharp disapproval on his face. "Some new form of amusement, I suppose. I don't think I like the looks of it."

"Now, Walter," Rita soothed.

"Don't stew, Walter," Grandfather told him. "And don't wear a hole in the floor. Pull up a chair and sit a spell. This may prove to be interesting."

"Why didn't someone pop some corn?" Rita asked. "Or make a batch of fudge. Gee, some fudge sounds good, with lots and lots of walnuts."

"For Pete's sake, Rita," Walter muttered. "Can't you think about anything but eating?"

"Don't be so grumpy, Walter. Maybe something exciting's about to happen."

Walter glared at her and continued to eye Doug and me suspiciously. Conversation tapered off and they all watched us steadily, each with a distinctive expression. Grandfather was nonchalant, Walter suspicious, Leslie bright-eyed, Rita wide-eyed, Nina inscrutable. The calico cat had gone to sleep. She opened one eye, decided she wasn't missing too much, and closed it.

At length the cupboard was bare and we sat among wild clutter.

Doug rubbed his chin. "I could do with a flashlight," he said.

I surveyed the clutter, then reached behind an opened cupboard door and granted his request.

"Oh, good girl," he said. "What would I do without *you*?" He flashed the light all about the interior and peered inside.

I peered, too.

"What are you up to?" Walter demanded. "Dad, you ought to put a stop to this."

"Oh, hush, Walt," Rita said. "Let's wait and see what happens. It's some sort of surprise. I like surprises. We don't have enough around here."

"If you ask me, we have too many," Walter replied.

Doug appeared deaf to his words. He was meticulously examining the individual pieces of wood that constituted the cupboard and seemed bemused by nail heads visible in the back sections. He extended an inquiring finger to one of the little round heads. "Got a hammer with a nail puller, Cyrus?" he asked.

"Why, son, I didn't run a hardware store half my life only to reach my old age bereft of the simplest tools. Of course, I've got a claw hammer, but not on me." Slowly, Grandfather stirred and pulled himself to his feet.

"Sit down," Walter said. "I know where it is."

Moments later, Walter came back into the den, hammer in hand. His look was grim and I wouldn't have been surprised if he had thrown the tool at Doug. But he did not. He merely shoved it roughly forward and accompanied the procedure with a thoroughly surly look.

The nails were not large ones and soon Doug had carefully pried them from the wood. He held one of them up to the light and studied it with curiosity. Once again, he examined the boards of the cupboard, pushing at them with the palm of his hands. Nothing happened. Undaunted and with half his body inside the interior, he continued to peer, poke, and examine.

My own confidence was slipping. Softly I said to him, "We may have to take out the paneling on the other side of the wall."

"It may come to that," he admitted, continuing the methodical search. "But I hope not."

The others grew restive. Legs were crossed and uncrossed, positions changed, and sighs were exhaled.

I couldn't bear to face the possibility that our efforts might come to nought. Since first I had chanced to wonder about the paneled chimney wall of my bedroom, a powerful drive had spurred me on. I didn't know what had spurred Doug on, but we did seem to be operating on the same wave length.

I had pondered about the big chimeny that came up through the center of that side of the house. In my room the space on the left of the closed-up fireplace had been utilized as a clothes closet. Staring blankly at the wall, I began to wonder why the builder had not utilized the space on the other side for a second closet or built-in cabinet or even a wall recess that would afford space for a bureau or the like. I thought about the layout of the house. The attic above, Grandfather's room below, with its identical paneled fireplace wall, on the other side of which was the den with its big corner cabinet.

Half of Doug's body was still squirming inside the cupboard, while I focused the flashlight for him. He was fiddling now with a small block of wood set low in the corner, near the floor of the cupboard. Again, he asked for the claw hammer and tried it to no avail.

"You got some kind of nippers?" he asked Grandfather.

Walter rose to fetch the tool, although he did it with no more joy than he had exhibited before.

Doug labored with the nippers and succeeded in pulling out several slender, almost headless nails. He fiddled some more with the block of wood. It seemed to want to move. He applied more pressure and the block did move downward just a fraction of an inch.

My heart began to thump…and the block slowly slid downward with a soft sound. Doug touched his palm to the back section on the

right It swung away from the wall at the

bottom.

He looked at me and I at him. My fingers that held the flashlight were trembling.

Then the others were gathering around, alerted by the excited silence emanating from the two of us. A look over my shoulder revealed a cluster of wide-eyed faces. Everyone seemed startled.

"What have you found there?" Walter demanded. Beads of perspiration had sprung out on his forehead.

"I think it's some kind of secret compartment," Rita said.

"Why, don't that beat all," Grandfather said.

"Oh, my word!" Leslie exclaimed. "Why, whatever is it for?"

The back section of the cupboard was raised further and Doug was wriggling his large frame into the space behind.

Once he was inside that secret area, I handed him the flashlight. "What do you see, Doug?" I asked.

"It's a staircase, of sorts," he said matter-of-factly.

"Oh—where does it lead to?" Rita asked.

"I'm trying to find out," Doug said. He was out of sight now. "It comes from below, from the basement."

"There's no opening into the basement," Walter said. "Those walls are solid concrete block."

I, for one, thought Walter was absolutely right.

We could hear movement inside. Then the back section lifted somewhat and the glow of the flashlight could be seen. "There's no way out down there, I don't think," Doug said.

"It would have been covered over years before," Walter said. "What are you trying to prove?"

Doug ignored him, calling out instead, "The steps go on up. I'm going to see where they lead to." His voice sounded strangely disembodied.

I thought I knew where they led to. Still, I

couldn't resist. I was pushing up the back section and crawling into the long-lost passage myself. "What are you finding, Doug?" I called out.

He flashed the light down, and I had a view of the little hidden staircase, which was cobwebby, splintery, and smelled of old wood long closed up. The passage was entirely enclosed and surely was little more than two feet wide, my eyes measured. The staircase consisted of rough plank steps without risers.

I stood still as Doug went farther up and fumbled with the floor of the room above his head. He was having difficulty, and I thought tools might be called for. A cacophony of chatter reached my ears from the den. I could hear Rita crying out, "But what does it mean? What does it mean?"

Doug and I knew what it meant.

Then Doug was pushing up some boards after a good deal of pounding. A light shone down on me. "Come on up, if you want."

I did want.

"But watch your step," he called down.

"I will." And I did oblige him, taking my time, touching the walls on either side of me in lieu of a banister. With my slender frame, passage wasn't really difficult, but I pitied any portly individual who might have made this particular climb or descent.

I was nearly overcome by a powerful affinity for the people of earlier days who had used this staircase, used it in life-or-death situations. I could almost hear heartbeats and hushed breathing, almost sense the various emotions that permeated the chamber all those many years ago. There must have been a multitude of them—fear, relief, hope, joy, thankfulness. I felt as if the spirits of those people still resided there and still experienced the myriad emotions.

Doug extended a hand to me at the top. "Welcome to Jacob's ladder," he told me. There were cobwebs in his hair.

I stepped out into the attic, warm and dimly lit, its only illumination being the sparse light of the ventilation openings and the bright halo of the flashlight beam.

I marveled. Grandfather had been right. The man who had built the house had known exactly what he was doing. He had known it with a mighty certainty. "I can't believe this, Doug. Tell me I'm not dreaming."

"Oh, no, you're not dreaming." Playfully, he chucked me on the chin. "But first things first," he said. He started to say something else, but voices and footsteps were sounding at the door to the attic.

The door was flung open, letting in rays of daylight.

"Oh, Daddy, just look!" Leslie exclaimed.

"I can see," Grandfather was saying. "But I'm not quite sure I believe it." He trod the joists cautiously.

"It's exciting," Rita gushed. "Just like what you'd see on television. A secret passageway. Oh, what was it used for? Do you think it was used for smuggling, or hiding home brew from revenuers? What are you doing? What is that?"

Rita's numerous questions fell on deaf ears. Doug was intent upon the trap door he'd just raised up. He trained the flashlight on the rough old plank piece. "Now just look what we have here."

I was at his side, hunched down on my knees. The others bunched around and peered over our shoulders.

It really was an unexpected find. Jacob Schumacher had kept a running tally. With a sharp knife or chisel he'd notched out neat little groups of five in neat little rows.

Doug was counting, *"Five, ten, fifteen, twenty…ninety-five, ninety-six, ninety-seven, ninety-eight."*

"He was a busy man, wasn't he?" I said.

"Yes," Doug answered, "and methodical."

"Such a shame he didn't get two more," I said, "just to make it a nice, even sum."

"I still don't understand what it means," Rita said.

Walter looked unhappy. He shook a finger at Doug. "I know what you're trying to do," he snarled. "You're trying to pin that killing on me."

Doug gave him a cool, steady look.

The portent of the discovery seemed at once to soak into everyone else. A secret way out of the den, after all, negating the closed-door aspect of the killing of Sam Roberts. Obviously, Walter had been thinking of it right along.

"You're not getting away with it," Walter went on. "Just because I was upstairs, now you're going to make everyone think I did it and then climbed up that passage. I never knew about that old passage. I didn't kill Sam Roberts, and I'm not taking the blame for it."

Walter reached into his pocket. For an awful moment or two I thought he might withdraw a knife or a gun. We seemed suspended in time. But Walter produced only a handkerchief and proceeded to mop his dripping brow.

A silence fell over all of us. Doug looked from face to face, carefully, methodically, lingeringly. He came back to Walter. "So you say you didn't do it, huh?"

"No!" Walter cried. "I didn't. I swear I didn't."

The vision of little marionettes was coming back to me, but this time it had a different twist. The scenario had changed. The door and locked window no longer counted for much. The picture was becoming much clearer. An awful realization was coming to me. I wanted to blot the picture from my mind but couldn't. Now I knew what it was I had heard that was pertinent but couldn't recall. Why did it have to turn out this way? This wasn't what I had wanted at all.

Doug spoke very softly now. "I say you didn't, either."

Walter's jaw sagged.

All eyes were on Doug. He pivoted a half turn and faced one of us squarely. "I say Walter didn't do it." He paused, then went on with what seemed a great reluctance. His words were just barely audible. "He wasn't the one who saw the man in brown, was he, Nina?"

Nina caught her breath and seemed to shudder. Her eyes blinked rapidly. Slowly she shook her head, back and forth. "No," she said at length, with a good deal of dignity, "no, he wasn't."

Everyone was staring at her and trying to assimilate the fact that she had, for all practical purposes, confessed to the killing of Sam Roberts.

I'd realized it just moments before. An assortment of facts had assailed me all at once. Nina was upstairs, but no one had seen her go up there. And a fragment of conversation flew back to me. Nina had said…most people wouldn't know what went on twenty-five years ago, *let alone a hundred forty years ago…*.

On the missing page it had said Jacob Schumacher was believed to have built his house around 1840. That would make the house around one hundred and forty years old. Other fragments of conversation came to me, fitting in here and there like puzzle pieces.

But why, oh why, did it have to be this way? "Oh, Nina! I didn't want this to happen!" I wailed.

"There, there," she said.

She remained calm, clasped her hands together, and looked at all of us without seeming to actually see us. "I'm sorry," she said. "I made it up about the man in brown because I didn't want Richard to be found guilty. Believe me, if he had been, I would have confessed. I should have anyway. I just didn't want to go to prison. I'm sorry." To steady herself, she reached out to one of the big chimneys.

"Why, Nina, why did all this happen?" Grandfather asked. "Why did you do it? I know you had a reason."

She sighed. "Yes, I had a reason." She paused, and we waited. "I saw him get out of his car and walk to the house that day. I recognized him, Sam Roberts. I had lost all of my savings to one of his schemes just before I came back here and went to work for you. After Leslie went out the back door to look for Richard, I came in the front door, went to the den, and closed the door behind me. I said, 'So you're the one who's causing all the trouble here. No wonder things are in an uproar.' Something like that.

"I told him it would do me good to tell the Calvins what he really was. He—he—" She began to tremble slightly. "He didn't seem concerned. Just sneered. He told me to keep my mouth shut or he'd shut it for me permanently. Then he grabbed hold of my arm and jerked it—twisted it. It was all I could do to keep from screaming. Well, when he hurt me, something just came over me. I was changed. It was like another person was inside my skin. He turned his back to me and faced the window on the side. It was a defiant thing for him to do. He said, 'Get out of here!' Suddenly, the poker was in my hand and I realized I'd just hit him over the head."

She shook her head and her sad eyes dropped to the floor.

"If you'd rather not go through all this—" Doug began.

Her hand shot up; her eyes lifted. "No. I want to.

It was just like I'd been in a dream and had just woke up. I realized exactly what I'd done. I leaned down over the man and just knew he was dead. I stood there for a while and began to feel very panicky. I wanted to get away. I wiped the poker off with my apron and went to the door and stooped down to look through the keyhole. There sat Leslie."

She paused. No one saw fit to prod her along.

"I saw that fancy letter opener laying there in the cupboard, and grabbed it and jammed it into the woodwork. I didn't want anyone to come through the door. I felt very strange. I remember exactly how I felt, but how can I explain it? I felt like I was in a daze, except I knew what was going on. That's not a very good way to express it. Suddenly, I felt like a condemned person facing a firing squad. It didn't seem to matter anymore. I wasn't frantic. I was...*complacent.* Then my mind was very clear. I was staring at that cupboard. Things came back to me that I'd forgotten, my great-grandmother telling me things about when she was a child, playing with a friend...in a big old brick house with a cupboard by the fireplace."

She seemed to have been transported back in time now. Her eyes had a faraway look.

She continued. "Her words came back to me just like they had been spoken the day before. I got down and moved things over in the bottom of the cabinet—it didn't have much in it then. I found the little block just like she said. I pushed hard and it worked. Then I lifted that back piece and climbed into the space. I couldn't quite get that bottom door to the cupboard shut from inside, so I left it ajar.

"It was so black inside the passage I couldn't see a thing, but I closed down the cabinet back and felt with my hands to see that the bars were in place and it was solid. Guess I wasn't thinking too clear by then. If I hadn't been able to find a way out right away, they'd have been looking for me soon.

"But that's neither here nor there. Something told me there might still be an opening into the attic, so I crept up those stairs. Sure enough, the trap door pushed up and I got out. I brushed myself off—the cobwebs and dust—as best I could and slipped out to the hallway, where I crossed and stepped into the bathroom. I had to get cleaned up better. Miranda caught a glimspe of me going in. At the time I didn't think much about the door being barred and the possibility that all the windows were locked. It turned out that it seemed like it was impossible for anyone to have been in the room. I didn't think anyone in the family would be charged. Later, I thought up the idea about the man in brown. I didn't want anyone to be hurt; I just didn't want to go to jail."

"Oh, Nina," was all I could say.

She turned to me. "I knew it was wrong when I didn't confess after they arrested your father, but I told myself: he is innocent; they can't find him guilty. I guess the jury believed my story. I was so thankful when they found Richard not guilty. The longer I kept my secret, the harder it was to think about telling the truth. I decided it was something I had to live with. One day when everyone was gone,

I drove some nails into the cupboard trying to make it more secure, and I put a lot of things in the bottom. Then I tried to nail down the trap door in the attic, but I guess I didn't do too good a job. I even went to the library and read books on local history. There was a book that told about a Jacob Schumacher. Then the other day I saw you carrying the same book."

She had lost the others by now, but she had said her piece. She untied her apron and took it off. It reminded me of a soldier laying down his arms.

Then Nina thought of something else that needed to be said. "I had to cut out that page, too, but I was beginning to realize it was about over. I'm sorry about that note, Miranda. I just thought maybe you'd go away. I regretted it afterward." A wry smile touched her melancholy face. "I couldn't very well write another note to say, 'It's all right. You don't have to go away after all.' I've been watching you. I knew this had to come. I've been trying to brace myself. I'm glad it's over."

Even Rita was rendered speechless by the unexpected revelation. No one said anything. We all went quietly down the stairs, except for Nina, who went to the upstairs room she occupied...to wait.

Grandfather, Doug, and I found our way to the kitchen.

Grandfather went directly to the phone. "I should have done this long ago. Better late than never, I guess. I wrote to Richard the other day. I hope he's received my letter. I'm going to call him now. Phooey!" He replaced the receiver. "I don't even know Richard's telephone number." He started thumbing through a notebook by the phone. "Doug wrote it down. Where did it go to?"

"I'll give it to you, Grandfather," I said. "Dad's probably at work right now. I'll give you his business phone number." And I did.

Then Doug and I walked toward the front door. We stopped and I brushed the cobwebs out of his hair and the dust off his natty suit. "You'd better just make up a story to explain your absence this morning, Doug," I told him. "The big cheese will never swallow the true story."

"Well—it's like this, sir—"

"You'll have to go to the police, won't you?" I asked. "It's over and I'm devoid of feeling. I've dreamed of this day and thought I'd be celebrating. I'm afraid it may have been a Pyrrhic victory. You'll help Nina, won't you, Doug?"

"Yes. But the truth needs to be told," he said simply. "Murder will out, as the man said. It's out of our control. I'll do everything I can to help her." He paused and looked reflective. "There are other truths needing to be told. I'll get around to them later." He reached down and kissed me lightly.

It had been some day. I felt a little dizzy.

"Hang on. I'll be coming round presently," he said. "We'll talk about things, lady with the deep gray eyes."

I smiled and watched him walk to his car and drive away.

There would be unpleasantness yet for a time, but the future did look brighter. Visions of little marionettes promised to be a thing of the past.

Jacob's Corner had a fascinating history. There was much more to be learned about it and the farmer who went all out in support of the cause he believed in and left a written record of sorts in the form of neat little rows of marks chiseled into the trap door which must have served him very well.

There would be much curiosity about the deftly constructed little passage. People would be clamoring to see it, and Grandfather would shake his head and bemoan the invasion of "fool sightseers." But I rather suspected he'd secretly relish the attention.

The unpleasantness would pass, surely. Perhaps the family would be reunited. And I'd do that painting. I had a genuine feel for the house now and its legacy from the past. I'd do a watercolor, I thought, and I'd breathe life into it as in nothing I'd ever done before.

I thought about Doug then, and how kind he was. I was glad I'd never gotten seriously interested in anyone else.

Made in the USA
San Bernardino, CA
18 November 2013